MISADVENTURES
WITH A
FIREFIGHTER

MISADVENTURES

WITH A

FIREFIGHTER

BY
JULIE MORGAN

WATERHOUSE PRESS

ISBN: 978-1-64263-208-8

To Meredith Wild… Thank you for believing in me and my story of Noah and Cara. You've completely changed my life. Thank you will never be enough.

CHAPTER ONE

CARA

My red-bottomed Louboutin pumps struck the tiles of my condo with every step, and the pearlescent glimmer of the shoes sent shards of light dancing across the floor. They were my absolute favorite pair. I wore them with a flimsy red dress that haltered around my neck.

It was the last week off before school started, and as a kindergarten teacher in New York City, I needed one last weekend of partying before grades, glue, and crayons became my life. I had sent a few texts out to friends, and the plan was to hit a new club that had recently opened.

I put on the teacherly persona of a good woman with great morals—an upstanding citizen. And I was. But don't get me wrong, I wasn't *that* person. I didn't wear Miss Librarian clothes by day and transform into a BDSM goddess at night. Not that I wouldn't... I mean, I'd try anything once. But it would be awkward if I ever ran into one of my student's parents. That was something I'd never want to experience. Also, I didn't carry around a paddle to spank someone who was out of line. Although some men I had met surely deserved it.

Like Jeremy Quill, my self-proclaimed first love who I'd thought I wanted to spend the rest of my life with. Bastard. We had been living in Tennessee when we met, and soon after, he had accepted a job transfer to Manhattan. When he'd asked me to move here, I knew marriage would follow. Until I moved here and caught him with another woman.

But that was eight years ago. I'd since settled down in Manhattan in my own apartment with the only man in my life I cared about: my cat, Luci, short for Lucifer. He was black, with a pink nose and hazel eyes, and had two small white spots on his head that were shaped like horns. He was sweet and affectionate toward me but hated everyone else. I kind of liked it that way.

I couldn't see myself settling down again. Not after what happened with Jeremy. My heart was locked, and I had thrown away the key.

Being single meant no one to report to, no one to worry about, no one to nag because they didn't pick up their clothes, or food, or plates, or anything. No one to judge me if I baked a batch of brownies at three a.m. and ate the entire pan.

I was the center of my own world. Did it make me shallow? Probably. Was I happy? Absolutely.

My phone buzzed on the kitchen counter, and my heels echoed in the silence of my home as I made my way toward it. Erin Malone's name appeared on the screen.

"Hey, Erin."

"Hey, yourself," my friend and coworker replied. "Are you ready?"

"Yep. Ready when you are."

"Okay, I'll be there in five," she said. "You know, I don't feel like our summer was quite long enough." I could almost hear a pout in her voice. "I'm not ready for a classroom full of new kids with snotty noses."

Erin and I taught kindergarten at the same elementary school.

I rolled my eyes. "Erin, come on. They're not so bad. They're still babies. And our future. They'll take care of us when they're older. Get on their good side!"

She laughed. "Getting on their good side means giving them a cookie when it should be nap time."

I grinned into the phone. "I live for nap time. Okay, enough of first-day blues. Get here and pick me up. I'm ready."

We hung up, and I placed my phone in my club purse. The small handbag was pearl in color and shimmered like my shoes. Cell, lip gloss, driver's license, some cash, and a condom. All my needed essentials.

The clock struck half past nine. The night was young, and soon I would be dancing in someone's arms. If I were lucky, my drinks would be paid for tonight, and if he were lucky, I'd be getting laid later on.

I was horny and single—a lethal combination. A predator on the prowl for her prey.

Running my hand through my long, straightened auburn locks, I checked my face once more in the full-length mirror by my front door. My creamy porcelain skin was perfect in this light and framed my caramel eyes behind long, black lashes. Everything still in place, I was picking up my keys from the counter when my phone vibrated in my purse. Erin was here. I headed toward the door, ready to get this night started.

◆ ◆ ◆ ◆

The bass of the music flowed through my body as if it was a fluid. It surrounded me, consumed me, became a part of my soul. Lifting my glass of wine, I tapped the edge to my friends' glasses.

"Here's to one of our final weekends before the school year begins."

"I should have been a teacher," Misty, one of our non-teacher friends, said. "I could get used to having summers off."

"Yeah, but you'd hate the salary," I reminded her.

"Well, for a teacher's salary, you wear designer clothes like you're rich," Erin added. "And I should know. We make the same fucking salary."

I laughed, then shrugged a single shoulder. "True, but my mom loves to buy me pretty things, and my family is rich." And they were. My father was an investor and knew exactly when to buy and sell. My mother claimed to be a Stepford wife until Real Housewives of Whateverville hit the TV. She'd thought of contacting the network to start up a show in our neighborhood in Tennessee.

"I hate you and love you at the same time," Erin said.

I smiled and took her chin between my index finger and thumb. "You love my money."

"I won't lie. It's nice, but it's not everything," Erin retorted.

"I beg to differ." I took a sip of wine. "My money makes me very happy. It's always there for me when I need it, it never talks back, and if I ask for something, it never tells me no. We should be announcing our engagement soon."

Erin laughed, then shook her head. "You should hear yourself sometimes."

I winked at her. "You know I'm only teasing. I mean, I do love having money, but I understand it isn't everything. After everything with Jeremy blew up, it was nice to know I was secure and didn't have to scramble. I could afford to get my own place."

"One day you'll meet someone who will make you second-guess having money as a first love," Erin said.

Maybe she was right, but in this moment, it was my cat and me, and I loved it. And my money didn't cheat on me. Nothing and no one would stand between me and my happiness.

Well, except for the man who just walked in wearing ass-hugging jeans and a white short-sleeved polo that revealed strong arms with a few tattoos. He was well-groomed, with sandy-blond hair. It wasn't long on top, and the sides were clipped short. He had a bit of stubble on his cheeks and chin, and when he looked my way, the bluest eyes I'd ever had the pleasure to stare into took my breath away.

He smiled, and a pulse surged through my body, like a light switch was flipped. *Turn me on and watch me purr for you all night.*

"I see the fire department is here tonight," Misty said. "Think they're taking a night off?"

"The fire department can't take a night off," Erin answered. "They're on three hundred sixty-five days a year. They rotate shifts so people can get sleep, but otherwise, they're never closed."

"I kind of want to set something on fire," I said.

Erin laughed. "The one there in a black polo." She pointed toward the men. "He's the chief. Hot, isn't he?"

I nodded. "Totally. What about the one in the white shirt?"

"Damn, he's fine," she said with a slight growl.

I had half a mind to slap her and stake claim on the man.

"I'm sure they're all together," she added.

"Good." I shoved the stemmed glass into her hand. "Hold my wine."

"Famous last words!" Erin shouted.

I stalked onto the dance floor, figuring if I moved toward

the group of firefighters, they'd take notice of me, maybe talk, maybe dance . . . maybe more.

Giving my hair a fresh toss, I made my way across the floor to the sound of cat calls from my girls. I couldn't help but smile. Rather than tearing each other down, we cheered one another on. It was how friends should be—non-judgy of whatever life decisions we made.

Have fun. Get laid. Sleep later.

The tempo of the song changed, and I moved my body to the beat, letting my hands run down the sides of my breasts to my waist. Lifting my gaze, I found his baby blues glued on mine.

Exactly where I wanted them.

Giving my best seductive smile, I leaned over just enough for him to view the crest of my breasts, and then I turned into a spin. Swaying my hips one way and then the other, I tried to imagine my blue-eyed firefighter on top of me, claiming my body. He reminded me of the actor who played Tarzan in the most recent movie remake.

An erotic visual came to me. Me, naked in his arms, as he slid his tongue up my neck and then nibbled across the sensitive area of my skin. His hands cupping my full breasts as he pressed my back to the wall. His leg would push between mine, and he'd lift me up, holding me against him.

I was startled and brought from my thoughts when a set of hands landed on my hips. Fingers pressed into my waist, and strong hands pulled my backside against his front. The person behind me felt tall, thick with muscles.

Before I turned to find out who the aggressor was, I glanced over to where my blue-eyed man once stood. He was nowhere in sight.

A smirk played across my lips, and I pressed my ass back against his crotch. Two could play at this game.

The heat of his breath warmed the nape of my neck. It sent a chill across my body, causing me to shiver.

"Are you cold, baby? I can warm you right up." My dancing partner's lips grazed the side of my neck.

I bit my bottom lip to keep myself from groaning in approval. When I turned around, it was him. The man's eyes were the depths of the ocean in a deep blue sea. He was taller than I'd initially thought. He had thick arms and a strong chest that was outlined underneath his shirt. When he smiled, his teeth were straight and beautiful behind his luscious lips. He smelled of an amazing male cologne, but thankfully it wasn't overwhelming.

I rested my hands on his chest, and his muscles twitched under my palms. "Do you promise to keep me warm if I say I'm cold?"

"All night, baby." He chuckled, and his smile was sexy. This man had a devil-may-care persona about him, and it was refreshing.

I grinned. I picked up on the slightest smell of soot that mixed with his cologne. Stepping closer into his space, I laced my fingers around his neck and pressed my breasts against his chest.

"What's a fine woman like you doing in a place like this?" he asked.

I pressed my lips together in an effort to not laugh. I had heard many pick-up lines, but nothing quite like that. "Is that the best you've got?"

He furrowed his brow. "Umm, what?"

"'What's a fine woman like you doing in a place like this?'

Seriously? You have to have better lines than that."

He smirked and lifted a brow. "Oh, really? Do tell, mistress. I'm afraid I must be schooled in the art of pick-up lines."

Yes, I liked him. He knew how to tease and take it. "Are your legs tired?"

"No, why?" he asked.

"Because you've been running through my mind all night."

He chuckled. "Nice. Okay, how's this? Damn, baby, are you an angel who fell from heaven?"

Since we were becoming pick-up-line buddies, I decided to fuck with him on this one. "What the hell, Karen. Are you suggesting I'm a fucking demon?"

His brows shot up in surprise. "I have no idea who Karen is, and no, I was suggesting you're an angel on earth."

I snorted through the laugh I couldn't hold back. "I may have to call you Karen from now on."

"Would you like to know my real name?"

"Is it a name you'd like to hear me scream out later tonight?"

A blaze erupted behind his eyes, and his lips pulled into a sinister grin.

Game on.

"'Karen' would not work for the things I would do to your body."

I slipped my finger over his lips, and he opened his mouth and lapped at the tip of my nail. "What is your name?"

"Noah Hughes."

"Hi, Noah Hughes. My name is Cara Murphy, and it's been a pleasure exchanging pick-up lines with you."

His grin was full of desire. His eyes dilated, and he wet his lips with his tongue. "I like a woman with spirit. I also like a woman who knows what she wants."

I raised my brow and leaned into him, my lips close to his. Close enough I could feel his breath fan across my mouth. "Do you know what I want, Noah Hughes?"

"I can venture a guess, Cara Murphy. However, I think it would be more fun to explore your body and find out together."

Truer words had never been spoken.

"Did you drive?" I asked.

He shook his head. "No, did you?"

"No, I didn't, but let me call for a ride." I pulled my phone from my purse, which was still strung across my body. "I have somewhere we can go that's not too far from here. Maybe a ten-minute car ride." I brought up the Uber app, ordered a ride, and then sent a text to Erin.

Hey, I'm leaving. See you at school on Monday. Love you.

I pressed Send and then brought the Uber app back up.

We made our way toward the exit. Despite my horny-and-single status, it really wasn't all that often I opted for a one-night stand, but for Noah, I was willing to make an exception. I didn't give my phone number to random strangers, and I definitely did not give my address. But with this firefighter, I was willing to forgo that rule too. Tonight, Noah was coming home with me, and I couldn't wait to get there.

CHAPTER TWO

NOAH

The best thing to come out of technology was the phone-a-ride. If you didn't drive or had too much to drink, it wasn't a problem anymore. Then again, there were still plenty of nights when we were called out to rip open a car that was mangled around a tree or power pole, sometimes with the worst-case scenario— dead on arrival. We always hoped no one else, like bystanders or other passengers, had been injured in the accident.

Tonight, though, was not going to be that night. Tonight was going to be shared with this beautiful woman, Cara. And if her lips were any indication of the rest of her, I was going to be a lucky man. Maybe I shouldn't have had the extra shot the chief dared me to do, but I wasn't one to back down. But I could feel the effects of it as the whiskey burned in my stomach, like a warm simmer from the embers of an almost extinguished fire. Then again, that could have been the effect Cara was having on my body.

The woman was sex in stilettos and a barely there red dress. Creamy skin and ginger hair, she was a goddess come to life.

It had been a few months since my last night of bliss, but tonight shouldn't be any different.

When I raised my hand to wave down our ride that

matched the description on her app, a four-door car pulled up and flashed their lights. The passenger window rolled down, and the man who matched the description of Nick, the driver, leaned over.

"Cara?"

"Yeah, that's me," she said.

I opened the back door for Cara. She slipped inside, leaned toward the driver, and verified the address we were headed to. She then watched me as I tucked in next to her. I didn't have much leg room, but I didn't necessarily care. I turned toward her and cupped the back of her head. "You're beautiful," I whispered.

"Shut up and kiss me."

And I did. Our lips met, and it was like an electric current shot through my body. Our tongues danced for dominance, and she submitted with a moan. Her lips were soft like velvet. She tasted of cinnamon and wine. I could devour her right here.

"Try to keep it in your pants until we get to your destination," Nick ordered.

I lifted my gaze to the rearview mirror to catch Cara flipping him off.

Hot damn, I'm in love.

I chuckled against her lips. "You seriously flipped off the driver?"

"Hell yes," she whispered. "He's ruining my game."

I smirked against her lips. "Well said." I feathered kisses across her cheek until I reached her ear. I flicked her lobe with my tongue before whispering, "I want to taste you."

She purred and reached between my legs. Cara rubbed her palm across my aching crotch and tilted her head back, exposing more of her neck for my consumption. "We're almost there."

Moments later, we pulled to a stop under a streetlight. Slipping my hand from cradling her neck to her shoulder, I nibbled on her ear. "Are we here?"

"Yeah," she groaned. "Let's go."

Nick cleared his throat, and as Cara stepped out of the car, I slipped a twenty to the driver. "Sorry for the show."

"Nah, man," Nick said and accepted the tip. "She's fucking hot."

"Yeah, she is, isn't she?"

Nick said something back that sounded like, "I'd hit that."

I closed the door behind me as Cara fished her keys from her small purse.

She turned to face me. "This is me," she said with a smile. She pointed her thumb over her shoulder toward the door. "Cold feet?"

I grinned and closed the distance to my lady in red. "Not a chance. Let's go."

She unlocked a door that led to an entry hall. White walls with four doors, mailboxes on the left, and a set of stairs, which we took up to the second floor. There were four more doors on this floor, just like the first. We headed to door number eight.

I stepped past her as she opened the door, and as she turned to close it, I focused in on her backside.

When she turned on the lights, the shadows defined her back and arms. She was toned and had a small pink-and-blue butterfly above her left shoulder. I took a step closer to her as she locked the deadbolt. My chest touched her back, and she held still, barely a breath leaving her.

I slid my hands up her bare arms and leaned in, my lips a breath from her ear. Her head tilted back against my shoulder, and she laid her hands on my hips.

"I need you," I whispered.

"Then take me."

With a rush of need, I grasped her wrists and held them above her head. Pressing my body to hers, I ground my erection against her ass. She groaned her approval and pressed back against me. I let go of her wrists and moved my hands to her breasts, giving them a firm squeeze. Her nipples hardened against my palms, and I had a sudden urge to suck on each of them.

In a quick move, I turned her to face me and pushed her back against the door. I slanted my mouth over hers and reached behind her neck for the dress closure. It wasn't tied behind her neck, as the material was smooth. I tugged it once, twice, then pulled on it hard until I heard the fabric tear.

"Shit, I'm sorry. I'll replace the dress," I mumbled against her lips.

"Fuck the dress," she whispered.

I groaned my approval and let the red fabric drop to the floor in a pile of crimson. Cara stood before me in nothing but a ruby naval ring, a black thong, and her heels. Her tits were stacked to perfection.

"Fuck me," I whispered and let the image of her toned body soak into my memory bank. Her body was something I did not want to forget.

"Get naked and I will."

I met her gaze, and she wore a grin that matched the naughty nature of her panties. Dropping down onto my left knee, I hooked my fingers on either side of the barely there fabric and brought the black material down the length of her legs. I grinned at the thin line of hair that led to her sex. She had a small birthmark the shape of a teardrop on her left hip.

She placed her hands on my shoulders and, one leg at a time, stepped out of her panties. She then kicked off her heels.

Her toenails were painted red, and a tattoo of a vine decorated the top of her right foot.

I lowered my other leg and sat back on my heels. Taking one of her legs, I lifted it over my shoulder and pulled her toward me. Her sex spread open for the taking, and I didn't hesitate, licking her from pussy to clit. She held the back of my head and pulled me closer. I wanted to devour her, make her come, have her scream my name, then wanted her coming back for more. I wanted to claim this woman as mine, if only for tonight.

No strings.

Just pure, unadulterated, hardcore sex.

I sucked on her clit and pushed two fingers inside her. Her walls were hot and wet and squeezed as I pumped into her.

"I need you inside me," she groaned.

I pulled back and looked up into her eyes. Letting go of her leg, I stood and took a swipe across my face, then tilted my lips over hers. She opened her mouth, and her tongue shot directly into mine, seeking control. It wasn't something I would willingly give up, but for her, I may do just about anything.

She grasped my pants and undid my belt, then the zipper. I reached for the condom in my back pocket as she quickly pushed down my pants and boxer briefs. Helping her undress me, I removed my polo and undershirt and stepped out of my pants and boxers.

I ripped the condom open and rolled it over my dick. I needed to be inside her. Now.

Cara grabbed hold of my shoulders, and as I lifted her up, she wrapped her legs around my body. I reached between us and pressed the head of my cock against her entrance, then pushed inside her.

She moaned and tilted her head back against the door. With each thrust to her body, Cara bounced with a gasp.

"Oh my God," she whispered.

"I want you to ride my cock," I growled next to her ear.

"My room is the first door on your right."

I slowed my movements and glanced over to an open door. Perfect. I held Cara's body in my arms and, without pulling out, carried her toward the door. The room held a queen-size, four-poster bed with a canopy attached. I grinned, made my way over to it, and fell backward with a bounce. I laid my hands on her hips and pushed up hard against her.

She reached above her head, grabbed hold of one of the bars of the canopy, and moved her body in rhythm with mine. Her hips moved forward and back, like a snake charmer stroking the beast in hopes of hypnotizing it. Consider me spellbound. Her tits bounced with each thrust to her body. It was a beautiful sight. I brought a hand to her breast and pinched her nipple. Moving my other hand down to her waist, I wanted to give her more. I pressed my thumb to her clit and moved it in a circular motion. Faster, then slower, drawing another moan, another whisper.

"Do you want to be on top, baby?" she whimpered.

I met her gaze and grinned with a nod. "Yeah." Leaning up toward her, I pressed my lips to hers, then peppered a trail to her neck. I rolled us on her bed, bringing myself on top of her body.

I grabbed her legs and yanked her against me, then pushed her thighs toward her chest. Her legs bent over my arms, and my movements grew faster, more erratic. The feeling of her pussy walls clenching my cock would drive me to the point of orgasm soon.

She took me in deep. Her head was tilted back, and her mouth was open. She slipped her tongue across her top lip, and a moan erupted from her.

I leaned down and sucked a nipple into my mouth, teasing it with my teeth. I pressed my palms into the bed and thrust hard inside her. Her body bounced against mine, and she looked into my eyes.

Letting go of one of her legs, I fisted her hair, tugged her head to the side, and then slid my tongue up the sensitive part of her neck. Our bodies moved together in a rhythm of bliss and chaos. The closer we drew to one another, the harder it became to suppress my orgasm.

Cara slipped her hand down to her pussy and rubbed her clit with her fingers. Her legs were spread wide for my viewing pleasure.

And pleasure she brought—more than any other woman I'd been with in a long while. She wasn't scared. She knew what she wanted, and she let herself give in to the moment. All I heard were our gasps of breath, our bodies slamming into one another, and Cara as she screamed my name when her orgasm rolled through her.

Her pussy gripped my cock with each stroke, and I couldn't hold back any longer. Heat pumped from my erection into the condom as I yelled out, "Fuck!"

Cara sat up and met my gaze. Her chest rose and fell with the breath she fought to catch. Sweat beaded on her forehead and trickled down her cheek. It looked erotic as hell.

I pulled from her gently and sat next to her on the bed.

She swiped her forehead. "Thank you. No one has made

me orgasm with sex alone. Ever."

I raised my brows. "Really?" She nodded, so I continued. "I don't know if I should say I'm sorry or feel flattered."

She smiled. "Go with the latter, please. You know what you're doing when it comes to the female form."

I chuckled. "Well, thank you, then." I stood from her bed and pulled off the condom. "Can I use your bathroom?"

She nodded. "Of course. And give me your phone?"

"Sure."

She pointed to the bathroom entrance, and I made my way over and disposed of the condom. After washing my hands, I went back for my clothes, got dressed, and headed back to her room with my phone in hand.

Cara had pulled on a silk robe and tied her auburn hair into a loose knot on her head. Her neck was flushed from where I had kissed her. A part of me wanted to strip her naked and do it all over again.

I unlocked my phone and handed it to her. She moved her thumbs over the screen, then handed it back to me.

"Here you go. I sent myself a text, so you now have my number and I have yours. Can I call you for a quick bounce every now and then?"

I raised my brows. "Like a friends-with-benefits arrangement?" She nodded, and I smirked. "I'm up for that." I chuckled. I closed the distance to her and tilted her head up with a touch to her chin. I slanted my lips over hers with a featherlight kiss. "Good night, sweet Cara."

"Good night, Noah."

I turned away from her and walked toward her bedroom door. Pausing, I looked over my shoulder at her as her robe fell to the floor. Her ass, legs, everything was perfect. I grinned and turned toward the front door and left Cara and the perfect night behind.

Tomorrow I had to work. I sent up a silent prayer for no fires in buildings or cats in trees.

CHAPTER THREE

CARA

A week had passed since the night with Noah. The morning after we parted ways, I found something left behind: his T-shirt. I had meant to wash it with my laundry but instead had placed it on my dresser. If there was a chance of getting it back to him, I would. Of course, that was assuming we saw each other again. If I had any say in it, we would.

I picked it up, brought it to my nose, and inhaled his scent—his body, his cologne, and the telltale trace of the smell of ashes. Since he was a firefighter, I guessed soot was something that came with the territory.

Regardless, school would start tomorrow, and Noah would be nowhere to be found—unless I started a fire. I grinned at the thought.

Well, hey there, good-looking. Happy to see you saw my smoke signals. Oh, and here's your shirt.

I decided today's outfit would be a black dress with a flower pattern and ballet slipper shoes. I braided my hair so it settled over my left shoulder, swiped lip gloss over my lips, and grabbed my messenger bag.

I looked at Noah's T-shirt once more. With a sigh, I picked it up, inhaled again, and set it back down before grabbing my keys and heading for my car. School would be in session tomorrow, and I needed to be sure I was ready for the big day.

♦ ♦ ♦ ♦

"Happy last day before first day," Erin, my kindergarten colleague, announced as we entered our school for one last run-through. Together we were an unstoppable team of snacks, stories, and naptime.

"Hey! Yeah, let's get ready for the craziness that is our life. Are you ready to rock?"

She nodded and walked in step with me. "Yeah. My classroom is ready."

"I read through my student files for the year," I said. "I'm hoping for a quiet year and no family drama."

Last year, a boy in my class had been picked up by child protective services. He had come to class with bruises on his wrists, arms, and legs. When I asked him what had happened, he shied away from the truth. I spoke with our school psychologist, and she was able to get more information from the child, which resulted in the authorities being called in.

From what I understood, the child was placed with his aunt and uncle in another state, and his parents lost their rights.

The hardest part of being a teacher was advocating for a child in an abusive situation. It wasn't that I didn't want to do it. It was the anguish the child had been put through. No one deserved that, especially a child.

"See you soon," Erin called as she made her way down the hall.

I opened my classroom door and stepped inside. It was quiet except for the sound of my shoes on the linoleum. The floor had recently been polished, and a colorful new mat had been laid out for the children, with different colors depicting different feelings and words. Sometimes they knew what the words meant; other times they just enjoyed looking at them.

I set my purse on my desk, sat down, and pulled my keyboard toward me. Tapping a few keys caused the computer monitor to come to life. I liked to do research on my students so I could learn a bit about them before meeting them. If I had one of their older siblings—and they had been a hellion or an angel—I'd know what I might be walking into. Same with students on an Individualized Education Program, or an IEP.

As I finished up researching the last student, I glanced out my room window to the playground. In the near distance, a man was mowing the grass by the monkey bars, and I stood from my desk and made my way over to the window. When he reached up to wipe the sweat from his brow, he reminded me of Noah.

The other night rushed to my mind and sent me back to the moment I took him home. His mouth on my body, the way he possessed me. Heat rushed from my cheeks to between my thighs.

A grin tugged to the corners of my mouth. I pulled my phone from my purse, swiped my finger to unlock it, and pulled up Noah's phone number to send him a text.

Hey, good-looking. You busy tonight?

I smiled when the moving ellipsis bounced as he typed.

I am now. What time, beautiful?

A giggle escaped me, and I shook my head at myself. We were just friends with benefits. I knew better than to get attached to someone who didn't want me for anything else.

How about 7 pm? Meet me at my place.

I set my phone down, made my way around the desk, and sat down in my chair. I was in a corner of the room and could see just about everything from this angle. No one could hide from me unless they were in the bathroom or supply closet. And my closet was huge. Erin had voiced something about being jealous of it. That she had been here longer than me, so she should have had it.

When my phone buzzed, all thoughts of Erin were replaced with thoughts of sex with Noah. I grabbed my phone and lifted it into view.

Sounds perfect. See you then.

I laid my phone on my desk, sat back in my chair, and smiled.

Hell to the yes.

Tomorrow was the first day of school, but that was the furthest thing from my mind. Tonight was all about quenching a heat I couldn't deny. My relief was on his way—a hot firefighter named Noah.

♦ ♦ ♦ ♦

Back at my condo, I took a shower and spritzed body oil across my skin. I slipped on a sheer, light-blue negligee with cream lace over the top and bottom, panties, garters, and thigh-high white hose. Snapping each garter to the stockings, I stepped into fawn-colored Louboutin heals that were opened-toed and encrusted with rhinestones. They were sexy on any given day, but with this outfit they were drop-dead fucking gorgeous.

Rolling my shoulders and smiling to myself in the mirror, I pulled my hair into a messy ponytail with a few wisps around my face.

Pure fucking porn mode.

The building bell rang, and my stomach flipped with butterflies and giddiness. My heels struck the tile as I made my way to the front door to see Noah's image in my visitor camera. I smiled and bounced on my toes.

Pressing the button to talk to him, I decided to have a little fun. "Yes? Who is it?"

He smirked and looked up to the camera. "I heard you had a fire to put out, ma'am."

I shook my head with a smile that would put the Cheshire Cat to shame. My heart raced when I pressed the enter button and he stepped through. Moments later, his footsteps grew louder as he made his way up the stairs, and I opened my door to peek through the crack.

Noah stood on the other side, arms crossed over his chest. A smirk tugged the corners of his mouth into a sexy curve set against his blue eyes. He wore a black T-shirt and jeans.

"May I come in?" he asked.

I stepped back and opened my door for him, keeping myself hidden behind the wooden frame. He stepped through and closed it behind him. We stood in silence, staring into each other's eyes. He took a step forward and touched my shoulder, then traced his fingers down the length of my arm.

"You look sexy as hell, Cara." He inched closer and tugged one of the straps of my negligee.

"Thank you." I reached for his shirt. "How long can you stay?"

"I'm on duty tomorrow. So for now? All night."

I grinned and pushed his shirt up. My hands slid over his sculpted body, the contours of his muscles ridged like a mountain range my tongue needed to explore. I reached up on my tiptoes and tugged the garment over his head, then tossed it.

"That's the right answer," I whispered as I pushed him toward my bedroom.

"You did all this for me?" he asked, gesturing to my attire. He pushed his pants down his legs, kicked them off with his shoes, and then fought to pull his socks off without teetering one way or the other.

"I like to dress up when I'm entertaining."

Noah's grin stretched in a crooked smirk. A wicked sparkle in his eyes warned me if I didn't move closer, he might pounce, pinning me to the bed. Inwardly, I laughed. *Bring it on.*

"Take a seat," I said as I reached for a pillow. He sat down on my bed, and I dropped the pillow to the floor. I lowered myself down and ran my hands up the outside of his strong, muscular legs.

Sliding my hands up the inside of his thighs, I pushed them apart and nestled myself closer to him. His cock was strong and hard, the head of his manhood a soft red that held a small bead of pre-come.

I leaned forward and slipped my tongue across the slit of the head of his cock, and the pearl slid across my pallet. Wrapping my hand around his shaft, I stroked him down, then up over his cockhead, and back down.

"Do you like it soft or rough?" I looked up to Noah.

His eyes were half-lowered as he contemplated his choice. "I'm not a fan of teeth on my dick, but if you nibbled, I wouldn't object."

I lifted a brow and grinned and then lowered my head and began sucking the tip of his cock like it was a lollipop. When I glanced up to him, our eyes met. He moved a hand to my hair and tugged it around his palm.

I took him all in, the head moving toward the back of my throat. I pulled on his cock, drawing a groan from my firefighter. As I came to the top, I sucked off his head with a pop of my lips.

"Fuck, Cara," he whispered.

Bringing my mouth back down over his shaft, I felt his dick throb. I drew him in again and pulled back, over and over, until he groaned out loud. My head bobbed up and down while Noah hissed and moaned with each stroke of my mouth.

Wanting to follow through with a little of the roughness, I nibbled on his head. He hissed and tugged on my hair.

"Don't bite me too hard, but damn, I like it."

I pulled his cock to the side and ran my tongue up his shaft. "Do you want me to nibble it more, or are you ready to fuck me?"

Without answering, he offered me his hand, and I took it. He helped me to my feet, then stood before me. He cupped my face with his hand and glided his thumb over my cheek. "You're beautiful."

"Thank you."

He leaned in, and with a soft, tender feathering of his lips, he kissed my cheek, then peppered his lips toward my ear. "I'm going to fuck you," he whispered.

"Oh yes." A shiver began at the top of my spine, and my body quivered in excitement.

Noah slid the negligee straps over my arms and let the garment fall to the floor. "I'd like to leave the stockings on, because damn, they're fucking hot."

"As you wish." I slipped my arms up around his neck.

He slanted his mouth across mine, and I opened for his tongue. He teased my mouth as if he were licking my clit. It turned me on, imagining him between my legs, sucking me to orgasm. His body possessed mine in a way that made me want to submit to this man.

I wasn't sure if it was his experienced, calloused hands, or his gentle nature toward me, or knowing he would run with pure adrenaline toward a fire—it was electrifying to think he'd put his life on the line for a complete stranger. That made me want him that much more.

"I need you," I mumbled against his mouth.

In a flash, Noah turned me toward the bed and bent me over. He ran his hand down the length of my leg, then brought it back up over the top of my ass.

"Get up there on your hands and knees. I want to see your ass in my face."

My pussy became drenched with need as I crawled across my bed. I looked to Noah over my shoulder and spread my legs.

"Fuck me, woman. You're fucking sexy as hell." He bent down, reached for his pants, and pulled out a condom, ripped it open, and slid it on. He came up on the bed behind me, lined the head of his cock to my pussy, and pushed in.

I moaned as he thrust, his fingers digging into the flesh of my body. Noah pounded into me, our bodies slapping against one another.

Noah picked up speed, and he growled. If a man in heat could make sounds for a mating call, that would be it. The raspiness of his voice sent me further down the rapid spiral toward an orgasm.

"Noah! I'm going to come. I'm going to fucking come. Fuck me!" The man deserved a fucking medal.

"Cara..."

He groaned my name. I wasn't sure if it was the tone of his voice or the fact that he said my name with such gruffness, but I shattered. I pushed back against his thrusts, taking as much as he was giving.

Noah came then, and his body grew rigid. His fingers dug harder into my flesh, and his hands shook. "Fuck, woman. Holy fuck." He panted for a moment, then pulled out. He reached down and slid the condom off.

I turned toward him on the bed and grinned. "You're welcome."

He chuckled and stood up. "Let me toss this."

I nodded and sat up to check the time. It was getting late, and tomorrow was the first day of school. With a sigh, I stood and followed him to the bathroom.

He stood by the sink, and with raised brows, he met my gaze in the mirror. "Care to share what's on your mind?"

I couldn't hide my smirk. "Shower with me before you go."

"I don't have another condom with me."

I shrugged. "Who said we're having sex?" I stepped around him, opened the shower door, and stepped in. "You can wash my back." Glancing over to him, I traced my gaze over the length of his body. "I'll definitely wash all of *you*."

His cock bounced as if coming back to life. "Well, I'm game," he said with a chuckle.

Thankfully my shower was large enough for two people. Then again, if it were tiny, I wouldn't care. He would be in it with me.

Tonight would end on a very sweet note. Noah was a tour de force in the bedroom. It was just a matter of time before I saw him outside my home.

That was, of course, if we decided to take things to another level.

CHAPTER FOUR

NOAH

I should have considered myself lucky. There had been fires, but we hadn't been called out on a major fire in a while. Of course, someone would light something on fire, burn some legal papers, or worse—like purposely starting a fire. I had no patience for pyromania.

It was early Monday morning, around four a.m. The moon still held the light in the sky, but soon the sun would rise. The building before us was staged as a practice fire. It was old and condemned, out of sight from other areas of town.

We pulled up in the fire engine and exited in formation. Another firefighter and I grabbed a hose, pointed it toward the flames, and turned it on. Water rushed out in force toward the burning structure. Two others ran in through the front with their turnout gear, face masks, and axes at the ready. As they stormed inside, I could hear them yelling to each other.

It was a simulation, but everything was taken as seriously as if it had been a real fire on a real day with real people inside. In our case, they were only dummies.

In time, we began to extinguish the fire. Our chief walked with his clipboard, taking notes. We moved to the right and focused the water on another part of the building.

The first fighter came running out with a dummy in his

arms. He made his way over to the paramedic truck that always rode out with us. He placed the body on the stretcher, pointed out a few burns and bruises, then went back in the burning building.

The second fighter came through the door carrying a test dummy over his shoulder. It looked like a model of a child. It gripped my heart every time a child was part of a rescue mission. It made me think of my own son, Marshall.

He had just turned five and was starting kindergarten tomorrow. Thinking of his school, I called out to my chief. "Sir, the time?"

"You got somewhere to be?" he replied.

"Actually, yes, I do. My son's first day of school is today. I'd like to be home to make sure he's ready to rock and roll." I glanced over to my chief. The man was tall and had a thick build with salt and pepper hair cut short. He reminded me of the *GI Joe* action figure, Duke. When Marshall plays with his toys and brings out Duke, I chuckle and think of my chief.

"Understood. We'll be done soon enough to get you home and play house."

"You're just jealous," I yelled back.

"Jealous of what? Having a kid at home? Nah, that's all you, man. I'm not parenting material. I can barely stand you fuckers."

I chuckled and shook my head. As much as he teased, the chief meant well. He was there for me—hell, my entire unit was—when my world crashed down on me. When I needed my brothers, the fire department didn't hesitate. They were there for me in ways I could never repay.

"All right, ladies, let's wrap it up," the chief called. "As much as I'd love to run through another simulation, we only have one building we can tear up. Let's clean it up and go back to the station."

I closed off the hose, and we carried it back to the truck. We would need to inspect our dummy bodies, review how we did on the rescue, and make sure nothing was missed. In a few hours, I'd be home, Marshall would be ready for school, and he'd begin the first of many days as a student. My son was growing up, and I only wished his mother could be here to witness it.

◆ ◆ ◆ ◆

Arriving at my parents' house, I walked in through their front door and called out, "Hey! I'm here. Is Marshall ready?"

Marshall was five going on sixteen some days, while others he was my GI Joe-playing, Lego-building, blanket-fort guy. Everyone told me he was my spitting image, but each time I looked into his eyes, I saw his mother.

"Daddy!" Marshall came running down the hall toward the front entrance. His smile could light up a room.

"Hey, sports fan. You ready to go meet your teacher?"

He nodded, then covered his face. "You smell like smoke."

"Well, I put out a fire earlier, kiddo."

His eyes widened. "Did you ride on the big truck?"

I nodded and squatted down to his height. "Sure did. You know what else?"

"What?" he asked, his eyes lit with amazement and wonder.

"I'm working on getting your class a backstage pass tour."

"Oh, that would be cool, but we haven't met my teacher yet."

I smiled and rustled his hair. "You will today, son. Now give me five minutes so I can take a quick shower and get cleaned up."

"Okay. Remember to wash your butt!" He ran back toward his room that my parents had set up for him.

I shook my head and stood. *Remember to wash your butt.* Must be something he heard from his mom.

"Hey, son." My mom's voice came from the kitchen. The walls of the home I grew up in were lined with family photos and artwork from various stores.

"Hey, Mom," I called back. "Thanks again for keeping Marshall."

"No problem. He seems excited about school."

"I can't believe he's starting school." I pulled out a chair from the dining room table and sat down. A candle centerpiece sat untouched on the table. I picked up one of the candles and smelled it. Vanilla. "Autumn would have loved this."

My mom wiped her hands on a dishcloth, then walked over to me. She placed her hand on my shoulder. "We all miss her, honey, but"—she sat down in the chair next to mine—"have you considered dating again? It's been almost five years."

"I don't want to talk about this." My mother wanted to see me happy, and she also had this urge to fix me up on blind dates. It was enough to drive me insane. "I don't want to date anyone right now. My attention is on Marshall. I want him to succeed."

"And what about your happiness?"

I set down the candle and looked at my mom. "Who said I'm not happy?"

She lifted a brow. "I can see it in you, son. You're lonely. She wouldn't hold it against you if you were to fall in love again.

It's the natural course of action."

"Where'd you hear that from? Survivors Anonymous?" My father had died over ten years ago. My mom found a survivors group, and it seemed to have helped her when I couldn't. It's not that I wasn't there, but I think she needed someone not as close to the situation. Someone unbiased. Or maybe it was finding someone who had been through the same ordeal.

She smirked and shook her head. "You know that's not the name of it, but yes. That's where I heard it." She stood and made her way back to the kitchen.

A sweet smell perked up my interest and changed the subject. "What are you baking?"

"Cookies for Marshall to take to his new teacher."

"Can you do that?"

"Well, I can. Whether you can bake or not is the question."

I chuckled. "You know I can cook, but that's not what I was asking."

"Oh, I know you can cook, but you can't bake to save your life." She winked at me and opened the oven door. "Perfect." She pulled out a cookie sheet filled with fresh chocolate chip cookies, set it on the stovetop, and closed the oven. "I hope his teacher likes these."

"Yeah, I'm sure he or she will. All right, Mom, I need to clean up and take Marshall to school. See you this afternoon?"

"Yes, I'll be here."

"Love you, Mom. Thank you again for keeping him." I stood and made my way over to her, then kissed her on the cheek.

"Anything for you, son, anytime. Now go and get my grandson educated!"

♦ ♦ ♦ ♦

The traffic was insane. From the crosswalk to the front door, people were coming and going. It was a bit overwhelming. Then again, it was the first day of school. I recognized a few people just because I worked for the city. New York City was large, but at the same time, it was a tiny place on earth.

"Where's the office?" asked a woman holding her son's hand.

"This way," a person with a clipboard offered.

I looked down at the slip of paper with Marshall's name, classroom number, and teacher's name. Cara Murphy. I blinked.

There's no way this could be the same person I saw last night.

I looked at the room number once more. I pride myself on not having to ask for directions. We could do this without the stress of getting lost in halls.

Right?

"Daddy, where is my class?"

I looked down to my son, my mini-me who stood just to my waist. His sandy-blond hair was styled when we left the house. Now, though, it appeared like he just rolled out of bed. Messy was the new style, but later in life he'd appreciate getting cleaned up for a pretty girl. Well, much later in life.

In his hands, he held a tin of homemade chocolate chip cookies.

"We'll find it, son." I squeezed his hand. "Come on, let's go down this hall. You're in classroom 2A, and I see 4B here. Maybe the next hall down?"

"Okay," he said as we ventured forward.

Gray-painted lockers with locks were stacked two levels high. The all-too-familiar smell of school reminded me of my own school days. I didn't miss high school by any means, but if I could go back without having to worry about bills and adult responsibility, I would say hell yes. But now, with Marshall in my life, I wouldn't change a thing.

Two aisles later, I found room 2B and, across from it, 2A.

"Here we are, son," I announced, feeling a sense of accomplishment. The outside of the door was covered with red apples with the names of the students in the classroom, and in the center was Miss Murphy.

"I bet your teacher's name is Miss Murphy," I said to my son.

"I can't wait to meet her," he announced with a smile. "Can we go inside?"

"You bet. Come on." I turned the handle and pulled the door open. Marshall stepped past me and went inside. I followed close behind, pulling the door closed behind me. Curious about who Miss Murphy was, I scanned the faces of the children, their parents in tow.

One mother was crying and hugging her daughter. Another father stood with both hands on his hips, beaming with pride.

"Where's Miss Murphy?" Marshall asked.

"I don't know, son. I'm sure she's in here somewhere."

"There's her desk," he announced with excitement in his voice. "She's over there! Come on, Daddy!"

Following my son's lead, we made our way over to the teacher's desk. A nameplate with Miss Murphy sat on the edge of her desk, next to a laptop and a small vase with flowers.

"You must be Marshall," called a female voice.

"Yes, I am!" he exclaimed. "And these cookies are for you!

My grandmother made them."

"Wow, thank you! Is this your father?"

"Yeah, this is my dad."

I didn't turn around at first because, honestly, her voice was familiar, too familiar. She sounded just like Cara, the woman I was with last night and a week before that. I closed my eyes and took a deep breath, sending up a silent prayer to whatever being may be listening that my son's teacher was not her, not my friendly fuck, not my Cara.

I put on a smile as my heart slammed in my chest. Slowly, deliberately, I turned around until my eyes landed on her. Eyes the color of caramel and long auburn hair I had just run my fingers through. Ivory skin I remembered so clearly. She wore a floral dress that was fitted above her waist and flowed out just below that. It was cut just above her breast line, and she looked sexy as hell.

Her eyes widened with the same surprise I felt, and a blush rushed her neck and landed on her cheeks.

"Miss Murphy," I said in a voice that sounded much calmer than I felt. "Pleasure to meet you."

She stared at me for a long moment, and her mouth hung open. When she didn't say or do anything, my son touched my arm.

"Is she okay?" he whispered.

I kept my eyes focused on hers when I nodded. "Yes, she's fine. Right, Miss Murphy?"

She shook her head and closed her mouth. With a smile equally as forced as my own, she finally spoke. "Yes, Marshall, thank you. I'm okay. I thought I recognized your dad, but I'm obviously mistaken."

"Obviously," I returned.

She nodded and reached for Marshall's hand. "Can I show you where your desk will be?"

"Yes!"

"Okay," she said and met my gaze once more, then turned away with my son.

With a deep sigh, I rested my hands on my hips. How in the hell did this happen? My latest fling, the woman who held my interest, even if for a short period of time, was my son's kindergarten teacher?

Oh, someone sure has a good sense of humor to pull this one off. I feel like I'm being punked.

"Okay, boys and girls," Cara Murphy announced, bringing me from my thoughts. "Let's gather on the carpet and play Duck Duck Goose! Marshall, why don't you start?"

My son jumped to his feet and began tapping the heads of the other students.

Duck.

Duck.

Duck.

Fool. That would be me, the fucking fool. Who needs a goose when I can dress in a jester outfit and prance around like the idiot I am?

This would be my life. I meet a woman who may just be a fuck buddy right now, but damn if I didn't want more. But now that she's my son's teacher? She's completely off-limits.

Which made me want her that much more.

I managed to get a space in the room where other parents were not standing. Cara made her way over toward me.

"What are you doing here?" she asked.

I raised my brows. *Really?* "Well, it's the first day of school, and it looks like you're Marshall's teacher."

"Can I ask where his mother is?"

"Yeah, you can ask, but she won't be here."

Now she raised her brows. "Ever?"

I shook my head.

"Okay, well, all of this . . . it caught me off guard. I wasn't expecting to see you here, of all places."

"Yeah," I said and rubbed the back of my neck. "That makes two of us."

She lowered her gaze again and crossed her arms over her chest. She leaned in and whispered, "Last night shouldn't have happened. We need to be professional for the kids and for my career here at the school. You don't know me, and I don't know you. Agreed?"

My chest ached. I barely knew the woman, but I'd enjoyed my time with her. I wanted more, needed more of her. I wasn't ready for this to be over. But she was right. This had to end, for the sake of her career and for my son's education. But what if we continued to see each other anyway? Well, time would definitely tell.

"Agreed," I mumbled and lifted my brow. "Under conditions."

She tilted her head. "There are no conditions, Noah."

I felt a smirk pull on my lips. "There are always conditions."

"Miss Murphy?" one of the parents called.

She shook her head at me and turned toward the other parent. I took this moment to make my way over to Marshall. I bent down and rustled his hair.

"I'm going to head out now. You ready to take on kindergarten, sports fan?"

"Yeah!" He stood and had a smile that reached ear to ear. He hugged me and then sat back down to continue playing. He was excited about school. I was ready for him to get started. But was I ready to face Cara Murphy as his schoolteacher when I'd licked, sucked, and kissed every part of her body?

Maybe I could convince her to one day wear a naughty teacher outfit for me while Van Halen's "Hot for Teacher" played in the background.

Challenge accepted. *Get ready, Miss Murphy. Get ready.*

CHAPTER FIVE

CARA

I once read that when you stare the devil in the eye, you shouldn't blink. If you do, he wins. However, if you persist and don't move, don't blink, you'll make him believe he's staring at his own reflection.

When I experienced my first night with Noah, I knew I would want him again and again and again. I'm greedy. I can't help myself. But today, when Marshall's father stood with his back to me, fear clamped on my chest when I thought it was Noah. From the back, it looked like him, but there was no possible way it could be. Until he turned around. I looked up into the eyes of the man who I gave myself to last night. It was like looking into the eyes of Lucifer. And damn was that man sexy.

Of all the schools, of all the places, of all the teachers Marshall could have possibly had, he had me. And his father was Noah Hughes.

I thought of Noah's lips on mine, on my body, between my legs. The way he owned me, controlled my body, and how he brought me to a whole new high I never knew I could reach.

And I'm his son's teacher.

With a groan, I sagged in my chair in my classroom. The students had already been released, and my teacher's aides had already cleaned up the classroom and called it a day. I could only think about Noah. He agreed we shouldn't see each other again, but the smirk on his lips and the spark in his eyes told another story.

He smelled of cologne, soot, and musky woods. And I relished in it. I still had his shirt from our first night together. I'd wanted to give it back to him last night, but I'd forgotten. What did I do with it now? Hold on to it? Throw it away? I'd made a point to him that we couldn't continue, that it had to end. I had to be careful. This was my career, and it was my year to finally earn tenure. No one—not even Noah—would get in the way of that goal.

However, outside of school, in my own home, would anyone have to know? I could invite him over for dinner and drinks . . . and sex. Oh my God, the sex.

Get ahold of yourself, Murphy. You barely know him.

I groaned and stood from my desk. Heat ignited between my legs as my mind continued to think of Noah and his amazing lips and tantalizing tongue. Oh, the things he could do with his tongue.

Stop it!

I needed to get Noah Hughes out of my head. I had to, damn it, for the safety of my job. Tomorrow I would talk to the principal about moving Marshall to Erin's class. It would be easier on everyone if that happened. I wouldn't get to know Marshall, there'd be no parent-teacher conferences with Noah, no visits, no nothing.

But Erin would see and get to know him. Is that what you really want? What if Noah falls for her instead?

I closed my eyes and tried to tell myself to shut the hell up. Who cared if Erin and Noah fell in love? Not that it would happen . . . if I had anything to do with it.

Gaah!

Sirens wailed outside, and I glanced over to the window. A firetruck sped by. Was Noah on it, on his way to put out a fire?

Hell, I have a fire he can put out.

I rolled my eyes at myself and grabbed my messenger bag with my laptop inside it. Lifting it over my shoulder, I fished my keys out just as a knock sounded on my classroom door. Looking up, I saw Erin.

"Hey," I said. "How was your first day?"

Erin came in wearing a light-blue button-down blouse and tan khaki capris. "Typical. Meet the parents, hope that the kids will behave through the year, parents reminding them to be nice and use their 'indoor voices.'"

"Oh, yeah. Same." I paused for a moment. Erin had started at this school a year before I did. We had been through a lot together, and I considered her one of my closest friends. I needed to talk to her about Noah to get her opinion on the situation. Hopefully, she'd give me some advice, or at least just listen. "I need to tell you something, and you have to promise to keep it to yourself."

"Sure. You can trust me." Erin crossed her arms over her chest. "What is it?"

"Seriously, this could be my job. I need to know my trust in you won't be violated."

She frowned. "What is it? What happened?"

I sighed and adjusted my bag on my shoulder. Looking to the ground, I felt my heart speed up. I shifted from one foot to the other. I squared my shoulders and looked Erin in the eyes. "One of my students. His dad is the firefighter from last week at the club."

Her eyes widened and mouth opened forming a silent *oh*, and then there was a long, painful silence.

"Say something," I said.

"What can I say? You know you need to request a transfer. If not for your own sake, for the kid's."

I nodded. "That's what I was thinking."

"But you don't want to, do you?"

I shrugged. "I've always been honest with you. I really like Noah. He's nice and just . . . damn. You know?"

"Is sex worth the job, though? You need to think of your position here with the school district. Once your tenure is under your belt, you can go anywhere, do anything you want. Are you willing to throw that away over a man you barely know?"

I lowered my eyes to the floor. She was absolutely right in everything she said. "No, I'm not willing to throw it away. I am, however, an adult. I can do this without letting him interfere with my head."

She shook her head. "You're making a mistake, but it's yours to make. You know I care about you, but Cara, if this firefighter breaks your heart, I won't be there to pick up the pieces. Consider yourself warned."

"Wow. Thanks, Erin. Love you too."

She rolled her eyes. "You know what I mean. Of course I'll be there, but when I say I told you so, I mean it. Get out while you can and make the change. Or don't. It's your choice."

I nodded. "Thanks for always being honest with me."

She winked. "You're welcome. I'm going to head home and soak my cares away in a bottle of wine and some bubbles. See you tomorrow."

"You got it. And wine sounds amazing."

As Erin turned to leave, my phone rang in my bag. I reached in and grabbed it and then glanced up to see that Erin had left my room. With a sigh, I looked back to my phone.

Noah Hughes

Do I answer it? I told him this needed to end between us, yet here he was calling me. A part of me wanted to shove the phone into my bag, but another wanted to demand an answer about why he was calling me.

The former part was stuffed back into my bag when the latter part answered the phone.

"Hello?"

"It's Noah. We need to talk."

His voice was like silk. It soothed an ache I had in my body—an ache only he could relieve. I closed my eyes and pressed my lips together.

"Cara?"

"Yeah, I'm here."

"Where are you? I'll come to you."

I squeezed my eyes tight and shook my head. "I'm still at the school."

"Are you alone?"

"Hell, Noah, I don't know. I'm about to leave. Did you need to talk about Marshall?" I was short and curt, but maybe it would help him to not call me. Who the hell knew.

"Not exactly, but I want to come up and see you. Don't leave. I'm a few blocks away."

Noah hung up before I could tell him no.

Shit. What do I do now?

I dropped my messenger bag on my desk and took a seat in my chair. I stared at my phone and contemplated what to do.

Do I leave and force him away, or go wait for him at the

school entrance? The doors were locked, and he'd need me to let him in.

Shit, shit, shit.

I stood and made my way out of the classroom and down the hallway to the front doors. The walk wasn't long. Kindergarten took up the first classrooms. When everything was so new, it was easier on the students to be closest to the doors coming and going each day.

Leaning against the doorjamb, I waited for a moment. What would he need to talk about that couldn't wait until tomorrow? Or for a parent-teacher conference? Hell, even an email? Our contact information was sent home with each student. All parents had our phone number and email. This meeting wasn't necessary, yet here I was.

Headlights broke through the darkness, and my stomach flipped with nervous butterflies. An SUV parked, and a tall male stepped out. His silhouette told me it was Noah. A fantasy scenario ran through my head as I watched him. It was raining, and we were caught out in it together. Laughing and running while our wet clothes clung to our bodies. He would lift me in his arms, twirl me around, kiss me, then make love to me on the ground while the water poured over our naked bodies.

Noah approached the school entrance, and I pushed the door open for him. He stepped through, wearing a red polo shirt with the NYFD logo embroidered on the left side above his pec. His jeans hugged his thighs. I wanted him to turn so I could see how they clung to his ass.

Instead, I smiled and motioned for him to follow me. "What brings you out?"

"Small talk?" he asked and matched my stride.

I didn't say anything until we reached my classroom. I

closed the door behind him, then offered him the chair next to my desk. Taking a seat in my chair, I turned my attention to the sexy firefighter in front of me. He smelled delicious—a scent I was growing accustomed to, one I wanted around me more often.

"Is it a good idea, you being Marshall's teacher?"

I lifted my brows. "Excuse me?" Offense flooded me, and I felt heat rise through my body as my temper flared.

"I want to make sure you won't be a bad influence on my son."

If my hair could turn into flames like a phoenix, I would engulf this man for insinuating such nonsense.

"I am not a bad influence. Your son is in capable hands with me as his teacher. If anyone is a bad influence, I would suggest looking in the mirror, Mr. Hughes."

He raised his brows at the formal use of his name. Good. I wanted a reaction from him because he certainly brought one out in me.

"If I am the worst influence here"—I pointed back and forth between the two of us—"then obviously you cannot handle your own vices."

He sat back in his chair and crossed his thick arms over his chest. "My concern is about Marshall and Marshall alone. I want to know that if he remains in your class, he won't be held accountable for anything that happens between us."

"Happens? Don't you mean *happened*? We are finished, Mr. Hughes." I shook my head and stood. "I will not jeopardize my career. It's time for you to leave."

"No." He stood and walked around behind my desk. "I'm not ready to leave. And I'm not done with you, Miss Murphy."

My heart sped so quickly, I felt it lodge in my throat. I

opened my mouth to say something, but only a squeak came out.

"And the way I see it," he said with a lowered voice, "you're not done with me either." Noah brought his hands up to my cheeks and cupped my face. His hands were warm and calloused. I longed to have them on my naked flesh, curling and pinching my nipples, his fingers inside my pussy while his tongue lashed at my clit.

A fire ignited between my legs, and I wanted Noah to extinguish it.

"No," I whispered. The word left my lips, and I immediately wanted to draw it back in. "No, we can't do this, Noah. Please."

He leaned in and pressed his forehead to mine. His scent of soot and cologne invaded my head and worked on me like a spell. My pussy was damp and my clit throbbed. All I had to do was look up. Our lips would meet, and he could take me right here on my desk.

Was that what I wanted?

With a nervous breath, I reached up and wrapped my hands around Noah's wrists. "We need to stop."

His gaze met mine. His eyes were dilated, and his lips parted. His blond hair was smoothed back, and I wanted to run my fingers through it. He stood over me, so tall above my small frame. It almost felt safe in his embrace. But he wasn't mine, and I wasn't his.

"Do you want me to go?"

I lowered my gaze to his chest, then to his waist. His erection pressed against his pants, and I had to swallow the saliva in my mouth.

"Do you think I'll be a good teacher for Marshall?"

"Yes," he whispered. "But I need to know he'll not be held

accountable if anything happens between us."

I met his gaze. "I can't promise something won't happen between us, but I can tell you that Marshall will never pay the price for anything you may or may not do."

With a growl, Noah reached for me and grabbed the back of my neck. He pulled me toward him, and our bodies collided with an epic explosion of sexual desire.

Noah claimed my lips, and it was then I realized I was starving for him. I needed him, more of him, in my life. Noah Hughes was a tall man, strong and beautiful. He was temptation hidden behind a secret door. And I was the key who opened that door and allowed him out to play.

This might be the best mistake I've ever made.

CHAPTER SIX

NOAH

I've heard it said that the best will come to those who wait. I feel as if I've been waiting for Cara to come into my life for a long time. I just didn't realize it until we met. She fit me like a fucking glove. Everything about her. Her personality, intelligence, amazing body, focus on her career, and willingness to venture into this friendship with me.

Her lips were soft and smooth, warm and welcoming. I imagined her lips surrounding my dick while I fucked her mouth. Fuck, it was a turn-on, and I needed to be inside her. However, looking around her classroom only reminded me of my son.

Turn-on went from high octane to absolute zero. If I ever needed to lose my fucking wood, this was how to do it. I pulled away from Cara long enough to look into her caramel irises. Her lids were lined with a black liner and set with long, beautiful lashes. She looked at my lips, then back to my eyes.

"What's the matter?" she asked.

"It's . . . well, it's this room. I can't do this with you in here while looking at where my boy will sit."

She giggled. "Well, I do have a closet that's quite large." Cara bit her bottom lip for a moment, then nodded. "We should go there. There might be other teachers still on the premises."

She pulled from my grasp and took a few steps back. "I can't chance losing my position here."

"I wouldn't want you to, either." I looked down to my hands and realized my palms had become sweaty. What the hell? Was I nervous? I ran into burning buildings, yet a woman had me on edge. "Look, something you said earlier. About us not doing this anymore."

Cara looked like a puppy that had been picked up to be adopted only to be put back down into the box where she was found. "Yeah?" she said in a soft voice just above a whisper. She clasped her hands in front of her fitted floral dress.

The last thing I'd ever want to do was hurt Cara's feelings. I hadn't gone out looking for someone. Maybe I had just been trying to jumpstart my libido again. But then I'd met her. Hell, when she just looks my way, I want to lean into her frame, surround her with my presence, and consume every inch of her.

Don't fucking do this, man. She's hot, and she's willing to be friends with benefits.

I took in a deep breath, and against everything my head was screaming, I went on. "I want to make sure my son will still get a good education here. I don't want anything between us, or not between us, to hinder that. My son . . . He's my life."

"Excuse me? Do you really think that low of me that I would take out any little-man-syndrome issues you're having on that incredible kid of yours? You really think that little of me?" She crossed her arms, a deep frown tugged at her lips, and her pissed-off eyes could have shot fire across the room. No amount of water would have helped now.

Way to go, asshole.

"Look, that's not what I meant."

"What exactly do you mean, then?"

I groaned and rubbed the back of my neck. "Cara, I just want the best for Marshall. That's all."

"I get that, but to sit here and come at me like that is not fair." She turned her back to me and lowered her head. "I think you should leave." She looked over her shoulder and lifted a brow. "And don't bother calling or coming over again. We're done with whatever this was between us."

It took a lot to piss me off, to get under my skin, but Cara Murphy found the flint that set me off. My arms shook as rage came over me. I stalked the few steps between us, and my chest rose and fell with the breaths I took. I grasped her arms and turned her around.

"Now you listen to me. Marshall has been through a lot. So much more than any other kid should ever have to experience. My job, as a father, is to protect him, first and foremost." The anger rose a little more as I leaned and towered over her small frame. I imagined myself as a lion about to ingest a small lamb.

Closing my eyes, I took a step back and pulled in a deep breath. "I'm . . . I'm sorry. Marshall is my world. I only want the best—"

"Stop. Just stop."

I opened my eyes, and she looked as pissed as I felt.

"I respect what you're saying about Marshall," she said, "but don't hold your shortcomings over my head."

My brow rose at her words. Slap meet face. "Well, all right. I'll make sure to never hold any shortcomings, or anything of the sort, over your head." I looked to the floor and shook my head. "You have no idea what we've been through." I met her gaze once more. "Maybe one day I'll fill you in, but today is not that day."

"What do you want from me, Noah?" Cara stepped closer and poked my chest with her finger. "You come in here demanding me to not hold Marshall accountable for anything you haven't even done. Are you going to think that every time I discipline Marshall—and I will have to discipline him from time to time, because every child needs discipline—that it's just me taking my frustration with you out on him? How is that fair to me? To your son?"

I pushed her finger away and placed my hands on my hips. "It's not fair, but what do women do when you date someone? You have baggage that always comes along with you. You will always hold the new person accountable for what the old boyfriend did. How is that fair to me?"

She raised her brows. "Wow. Okay, I didn't realize we were dating, number one. And number two, I have never done anything of the sort."

"Not yet."

"Mm-hmm."

A long silence fell between us before I looked up into her eyes once more. My chest ached, but I wasn't sure why. I didn't love Cara, but I did care for her. She was fast becoming a friend, not just someone I would fuck and leave.

Fucking without feelings, without emotions, was fun at first, sure. But what happened when feelings got involved? I'd been single since Marshall's birth and had never thought about bringing anyone into my life, or my son's, yet here I was having this conversation with Cara Murphy, my son's kindergarten teacher.

"Hi," I whispered.

She frowned and took a step closer. "I'm sorry. I don't think I heard you. Did you just say 'hi'?"

I nodded, then pinched the bridge of my nose. "Look, I'm sorry. I didn't mean—"

"You did. And I'd appreciate it if you'd leave those concerns at the door when you're with me. When it comes to your son? Different world. Regardless of what happens between us, it will have no reflection on him. You're welcome to request a transfer for your son if that would make you feel better."

I shook my head. "No, that's not necessary, unless you would advise it. It is your career this could affect." Stepping closer to Cara, I brushed the few hairs from her face behind her ear. "Please accept my apology."

She smiled, and it reached her eyes. "Of course."

With a sigh, I moved my arms around her slender frame and pulled her against me. She was warm, and for the first time in ages, I longed for the touch of a woman.

Not just any woman . . . Cara.

"Come on," she whispered and took my hand. She led me toward the back of her classroom toward a closed door. When she opened it, the smell of glue, crayons, and construction paper invaded my head. It took me back to my days in elementary school.

My teachers were never quite like Miss Murphy, though.

She flicked on the light and closed the closet door. She wasn't lying. The closet was huge.

Cara reached for my shirt and tugged at the material around my waist, untucking it from my pants. She stepped closer and ran her palms up the inside of my polo. Her hands were chilled, and my flesh rose with the sensations she sent through my body.

I brought up my hands and cupped her face. Tilting her head back, I leaned in and slanted my lips over hers. I moved one of my hands to cradle the back of her head, and in doing so, I grasped a handful of her hair. When I gave her hair a firm tug, she gasped against my lips. I slipped my other hand down her neckline to her breasts.

"I'd love to rip this dress from your body, but I have nothing you could wear to get home."

"I happen to like this dress," she teased. "Unzip me from the back."

I yanked her hair once more, and it drew a whimper. She closed her eyes, and her mouth opened as she gave herself over to me. Kneading a breast in one hand, I moved my mouth over her neck, licking the sensitive skin by her ear. "No, I'd rather leave it on."

She shuddered, and I felt her nipple harden through her clothes. I pulled the top of her dress and her bra down just enough to expose her tits. I lapped at her nipple, bringing the firm, stiff peak to a pebbled formation. Sucking on the taut skin, I nibbled it, then sucked it into my mouth before letting her go with a pop.

I let go of her hair and brought her back upright while I kissed her skin from the mounds of her chest to her neck and then laid my lips on hers.

Cara fisted her hands in my shirt and lifted a leg around my waist. "I need you," she whispered.

Fuck, I needed her. I needed to be inside her, Cara's body rocking against my own. I lowered myself to my knees and laid my hands on her hips. My eyes trained on hers, I moved my palms down the length of her thighs to her bare legs, soft and shaved. I moved my touch up under her skirt to her hips. Hooking my fingers into her panties, I pulled the garment down her legs to her ankles. She stepped out of them, and I set them to the side.

I lifted her skirt and took in the sight of her pussy. Bare and beautiful. Her slit was wet with need. Looking up to her, I smirked. "I'd love for you to ride my face, but I want that pussy on my dick."

Cara didn't disappoint. She lifted a brow, and with a smirk of her own, she turned around, spread her legs, and bent over. Her ass and pussy were directly in front of me, ready for the taking. My erection throbbed in my pants, begging for release.

Then, surprising me, Cara reached around and grabbed her ass cheeks and spread them. "Touch me," she said, looking over her shoulder.

"Fuck me," I groaned and pushed a finger into her pussy. Her channel was hot and wet, and her honey soaked my hand. I pressed my thumb to her clit and massaged it while I moved my finger in and out.

"That feels good," she groaned, "but I'd rather have you in me than your fingers."

With my free hand, I reached around and pulled a condom from my back pocket. I had brought one just in case. I'd had no idea how tonight would go here in her classroom. I had hoped to have sex with her at her place but never considered having it here.

"Rub your clit for me, baby," I said as I stood.

She did as I asked and massaged her nub with two of her fingers. She moaned softly and pressed her free hand to one of the shelves.

I opened my pants and let them and my boxer briefs drop. Ripping the condom open, I rolled it down my shaft and then took a few steps forward and pressed the head to her pussy.

She reached for my dick, grabbed it, and pushed back. With a slow thrust, I slid fully inside her. A groan of satisfaction left her lips. I pulled back and pushed in again harder. Cara gasped and, with both hands, held on to the shelves in front of her. I pushed her dress up over her back and gripped her hips in a tight grasp. With a hard thrust, I pulled her body back against mine, and our bodies connected like a cosmic force exploding, sparks ready to fly at any given moment.

"Fucking hell, Cara," I groaned. Her pussy squeezed my cock and then released, drawing every part of my life force into her. And I willingly gave it over.

"Harder," she whispered. The supplies on the shelf wobbled, and a few glue bottles and other items hit the floor. "Fuck me, Noah. Fuck me."

With a growl, I thrust harder and faster, our bodies in a perfect rhythm. I reached forward and grabbed a handful of her hair and wrapped it around my fist. I yanked hard, pulling her head back.

She arched her back. "Fuck yes. Fuck me."

"Come for me, baby," I said through gritted teeth. "Let yourself go."

"Shit," she cried, and a warm rush flooded my cock. "Yes, harder."

My orgasm rushed through my body to my balls and exploded inside her like a fucking fire hydrant. "Fuck yeah," I groaned and released her hair. I continued to thrust until my orgasm was spent.

Slowly, I pulled out, and then helped Cara stand upright.

"Wow," she whispered. Cara picked up the glue and other items that had tumbled to the floor and placed them back on the shelves.

I chuckled. "You're welcome."

She shook her head with a chuckle, then straightened her

dress. "Well, I suppose I should say thank you." She reached for her panties on the floor and pulled them on. "Earlier, when I said we should stop?"

I nodded and pulled the condom from my dick. Unsure where to put it for the time being, I laid it on the floor next to my feet. "Yeah?" I said as I fixed my boxers and pants back up around my waist.

"Forget what I said."

I grinned, picked up the condom, and took a step toward her. "I'm glad. You have something I can throw this away in?" I held up the used condom.

"Yeah. I have my own bathroom here. It's just outside the closet."

"Perfect." I left the supply closet and made my way over to the bathroom. I flushed the condom and then washed my hands. I looked at myself in the mirror and studied my reflection. As if judging myself for having an affair when there was no affair to be had.

What was I doing?

With a sigh, I turned off the water and dried my hands.

"Walk me to my car?" she asked as she picked up her messenger bag.

I turned around with a smile and nodded. "Absolutely."

We turned off the lights, left her room, and headed toward the exit. The hallway was dark. No lights except from those outside the building. There was no chance anyone was here or had heard us.

We reached the parking lot. "Wow, nice car."

She had a red Audi convertible with tan leather seats. How could she afford this on a teaching salary? There was much more to learn about Cara Murphy than I realized.

She smiled. "Call me thrifty."

I chuckled. "Sure thing. I'll call you?"

"You better. Or I'll come down to the fire station and raise hell."

"Oh, you would, wouldn't you?" I teased and pulled her into my arms. "Every one of the men at the firehouse would give their left nut to be with a woman like you."

"Their left nut, huh? How about you?"

I smirked. "I just gave you both nuts ten minutes ago."

She laughed, and it was a beautiful sound.

I tilted her head up with a touch of my finger under her chin. I slanted my lips over hers once more. "Good night, baby."

"Good night, lover," she whispered back.

When I let Cara go, she slipped into her car, started it up, and then sped out of the parking lot. I watched the red taillights dim as she drove farther away. With a sigh, I got into my SUV and started it up. A slight pang of guilt rushed over me, and I closed my eyes.

This was the first time I'd felt anything for anyone since Marshall's mother, and I had no idea what I was supposed to do with it. I ran my hand through my hair and rested back against the head rest. I closed my eyes, and images of Cara ran through my mind.

If this arrangement continued between us, we needed to set new boundaries, or someone was going to end up getting hurt. I refused to deal with another broken heart, and I would not break Cara's in the process, either.

With a sigh, I put my SUV into gear and started down the road home.

What the hell had I done?

CHAPTER SEVEN

CARA

This was supposed to be my year. The year when everything I had been working toward began to pay off. Since my first day as a teacher at New Expeditions Elementary, I knew I had found my home.

In addition to my kindergarten teaching, I had been working to become the head of the art department. I loved all things art, from finger painting to spotting an up-and-coming Monet, from ballet to music, from creative writing to interpretive dance—all of it inspired me in one form or another.

This year would be different, though. This year, I was one step away from being on top. Every step up had not been without a struggle, but it had been nothing I couldn't work through. Erin, my friend, walked the same steps with me. She'd shown an interest in the art department but ultimately had settled for science.

"There's nothing like a little friendly competition," I'd once told her. She'd disagreed and worried it would damage our friendship. *Only if we allow it to,* I'd told myself.

A few weeks had already passed since school started. Noah and I had only seen each other that one time, and of all places, that was in my supply closet. I can't get supplies without thinking about what we did in there, and I invariably leave blushing. We had agreed to be friends with benefits, but after finding out he was Marshall's father, one of my students, well, it wouldn't be in either of our better interests to keep this arrangement going.

Of course, that conversation was followed by mind-blowing sex.

"Miss Murphy?" Shayla, one of my students, called.

I pulled myself from my musings and smiled at the blond-haired girl. "Yes?"

"Can we start show-and-tell now? I'm excited to bring in my dog. My mom said she'd come in with Oliver."

I smiled. "Your dog's name is Oliver?"

She nodded and smiled through a missing baby tooth.

"I love the name!" I said. "Yes, we'll be starting shortly."

A moment later, there was a knock on my classroom door.

"Sounds like Oliver may be here," I announced.

My students cheered. Any chance to play with a dog, excitement ensued.

I made my way toward the door and opened it. On the other side stood a woman holding a dog on a leash. She was dressed as if she'd stepped off a runway magazine photoshoot for Ralph Lauren. She was wearing a tan trench coat and RL sunglasses, and her hair was styled perfectly.

Living in Manhattan had its perks, but sometimes people would dress to impress. I can't complain too much with my Louboutins I love to wear, which I wouldn't have been able to afford without my family's wealth.

"This must be Oliver?" I asked.

The woman chuckled. "Why yes, this is Oliver. I'm Emma, Shayla's mom."

I smiled and opened the door wide. "Please, come in and

make yourself at home. Students, please say hi to Oliver!" I smiled with my words. Oliver was a cute golden lab. His tail swung side to side, and he sniffed each kid who approached him.

I began to close the door when I heard someone clear his throat. "Oh, I'm sorry," I started before turning around. With a pause in my step and a skip in my heartbeat, I saw Noah standing in front of me, decked out in his firefighter gear.

I widened my eyes and opened my mouth.

He smirked. "Like what you see?"

I blinked once, twice, then frowned. "Is there a fire nearby?" This was all I could think of at the moment. I wanted him to put out the fire he caused me to feel every time I thought about the supply closet or my condo.

He chuckled and shook his head. "No, I'm here for Marshall. He asked me if I would be his show-and-tell."

"Oh." I blushed for an entirely different purpose. Why didn't I think of this? No, he wasn't here for me; he was here for his son.

Get a fucking grip, Murphy!

"Right," I said with a laugh. "Please, come inside." Noah stepped past me, and when I inhaled, his familiar scent of soot invaded my senses. I closed my eyes and inhaled once more, then turned toward my classroom.

Everyone's attention was on Oliver, and that was just fine with me.

I closed the door to my classroom and made my way toward my desk. The children in my classroom all had trinkets or knickknacks to present today, except Shayla's dog, Oliver, and Marshall's father, Noah.

I glanced over to my firefighter and watched him chuckle

at something Marshall said. He then looked up and met my gaze. He caught me watching him, and heat crept up my neck. He grinned and looked back to his son.

"Okay, so who would like to go first?" I asked.

"Me!" shouted three or four students. They waved their hands in the air, and smiles pulled their lips almost to their ears.

I wished we could hold on to this innocence as adults.

"Shayla, come up and tell us about Oliver."

I sat on the edge of my desk when Shayla squealed, "Yay!" She strode to the front of the room with her dog. She began telling the story of finding him at the local kennel.

I looked over at Noah once more, and this time, he was watching me. The man winked at me, and I grinned, my heart rushing in my chest. I lowered my gaze to my shoes and crossed my ankles, one over the other.

What the hell has Noah Hughes done to me?

Friends with benefits do not take things to the next level. Then again, there usually was no child involved, nor complications from a day job.

"Miss Murphy?"

"Hmm?" I looked over to Shayla. She apparently had finished her show-and-tell, and here I was, daydreaming about my firefighter. Her mother, Emma, hugged Shayla goodbye and then left with Oliver.

"Who's next?" I looked back over my classroom with a smile. I also squeezed my thighs together because I could feel Noah's stare penetrating me as if he were undressing me with his eyes.

"Marshall, why not come up and present your show-and-tell for us?"

"Come on, Daddy!" Marshall exclaimed and headed toward the front of the class. Noah followed his steps and glanced toward me with a grin.

"Everybody, this is my daddy. He's a firefighter for the FDNY. That stands for Fire Department of New York!"

After a few *oohs* and *ahhs*, Noah opened his fireman's jacket to reveal a fitted white tank.

Oh, the things I would have done to him if we were at my place.

Or in the supply closet.

Or if he had just rescued me.

"Hello, everyone. Miss Murphy." He nodded in my direction, and I returned the smile. "Who all knows what a fireman does?"

Many hands shot in the air, and Noah called on one student at a time.

"You put out fires!"

"You rescue animals from a burning building!"

"You get cats from trees!"

Noah chuckled. "Yes to the fires. Yes to the buildings. The cats, though, I have to say I haven't had to do that just yet. But I promise to send the story to class with Marshall if it happens."

"Oh, Miss Murphy," Marshall interjected. "Do you think we can do a class trip to the fire department?"

I raised my brows. "Oh, well, I'll need to check with the principal on that before we make any plans."

"Anytime you would like to come out and check out the fire station, you're always welcome," Noah said.

How much of "check out the station" was for the kids, and how much of it was an invite personally for me? Hopefully the latter.

"Yeah, let's do it!" one child yelled out.

"Do you have a spotted dog at the station?" another asked.

"Actually, we don't," Noah told them. "I wouldn't mind having a Dalmatian at the station, though. I love dogs just as much as Shayla there loves her Oliver."

"You could get us a dog," Marshall said.

Noah chuckled and shook his head. "Not us, no, but for the station. He would live there." Noah looked back to the students. "Did you know we are open every day of the year? We never take holidays off. We also train every single day there's not a fire. Maybe one day Miss Murphy can bring you out to a training exercise."

This request was followed by "Please!" and "Can we?" from several students.

"I'll see what we can do," I offered and stood with my hands out. "Now please, let's keep the noise level down, okay?"

"Yes, ma'am," said the students and Noah.

I glanced at him and wanted to giggle but decided to smile instead. "How much advance warning do you need to do a proper tour for the children?"

"One day at least, but we'd prefer a week."

"Consider it done," I said and walked over to Marshall. "Why don't you go find your seat."

Marshall hugged his dad and left Noah by my side. One by one, the students who had brought in their knickknacks showed their prized possessions to the others.

When the last student sat down, I looked to the clock. "It's lunchtime! Now if you'll please line up, the teacher's aides will be in shortly to bring you to the cafeteria." One by one, all the students left for their lunchtime, and the classroom grew to silence.

"Are you free for lunch?" Noah whispered in my ear.

It startled me since he was sitting behind me on a stool. I hadn't realized he'd stood or even moved. I pictured him in his turnout gear, minus the jacket. It sparked a flame inside my body that only he could put out.

I shook my head with a sigh. "No." I turned to face him, then continued. "I'm sorry. I have to grade papers and answer messages. But I am free tonight."

"Tonight? Good. I'm off today. I'll come by your place so we can talk."

I raised my brows. "So we can talk? Is this a good talk or bad?"

"Oh, no, it's a good talk. Don't worry."

I smiled with a nod. "How about seven? Do you like fish?"

"Yeah. You cooking?"

"I can." I looked out the classroom door when something caught my attention. It was Erin. She crossed her arms over her chest and shook her head. "Shit," I whispered.

"What is it?" he asked and followed my line of sight.

"Nothing. I'll see you tonight." I pushed past Noah, but he grabbed my arm. "Yes?"

"Are you sure everything is okay?"

I nodded. "Just swell."

He chuckled. "Who says swell anymore?"

I shrugged. "I guess I do."

He let go of my arm, then tilted his head with the fireman's hat on it. "Then I'll see you tonight."

I smiled with a nod, then turned back to my door. Erin had left. Would she suspect Noah and me of having an affair? And if she did, would she report me? No, she wouldn't. Erin was one of my closest friends.

With the silence of the classroom, Noah's steps were heavy in his boots.

"If I may ask," I started, "how much does your gear weigh?"

"Roughly forty-five pounds."

I widened my eyes. "Wow, I didn't realize it was that much!"

"Keeps us fit," he said.

I nodded. "I can attest to that."

He chuckled.

I closed my hand over my mouth and then pulled it away. "I thought that was in my head. I didn't realize I said that out loud." My cheeks burned, and I turned away from Noah.

He turned me back around and touched my cheek. "It's adorable," he whispered.

Noah Hughes towered over my body. He was long and lean but thick in all the right places. He was like a mountain wanting to be scaled, and I would be lying if I said I didn't want to try. Every bit of me wanted to latch on and claim this man.

He tilted his head, bent down, and pressed a kiss to my cheek. "See you tonight."

With that, Noah left my classroom. I touched my cheek where his lips touched my skin, and my heart leaped forward as if to race after my man in uniform.

CHAPTER EIGHT

NOAH

A few weeks had passed since the last time I had seen Cara. Then today during show-and-tell, she lit up the classroom like an ember burning on a log in the darkness of the woods. That one ember would be enough to burn bright, make a scar, and provide the perfect amount of light.

Cara was my ember. She could burn bright in the darkness, she could scar me beyond repair, and she could bring me back into the light.

I smiled, and my heart rushed to the rhythm of the excitement I felt. I smiled more, stood taller, and looked forward to when I would see her. For being a friends-with-benefits arrangement, this was becoming something more.

And it ate at me, hard and painful. It felt like I held my heart in my hand, then squeezed it until it exploded. It had been five years, and I still carried the guilt of Marshall's mother. I supposed I would no matter how much time passed.

With a sigh, I decided Cara needed to know about Marshall's mother, and tonight would be the night. Cara had become something of a beacon of hope, and it was time I did something about it. Because if I didn't, someone else would step in and steal her right out from underneath me.

She was an amazing woman. The way she worked with her

children but then turned off the teacher charm and became a sexy goddess of a woman. She made me want to drop to my knees and beg for mercy.

And I was not above begging. When it came to Cara, I was willing to do just about anything.

Grabbing my keys from the counter, I looked to the calendar on the wall and saw a red X over Monday's date.

"Crap."

Monday would be my day to volunteer with Marshall's class. I would be in Cara's classroom for a few hours... working. By her side. I would be able to watch her when she wasn't looking, but I couldn't touch. And God help me if we happened to pass by the supply closet or she sent me in to get anything.

I shook off the thought and headed toward the door. My mom picked up Marshall from school today and planned to keep him overnight. She had done so much for Marshall and me. I didn't know how I would ever repay her.

Mom had been here since Marshall was born. She'd become like a mom to my son—the only motherly figure he'd ever known. I was truly blessed to have her.

I headed out to my car. It would only be a matter of minutes before I arrived at Cara's place. Before I drove off, I picked up a pad of paper I keep in my SUV and jotted down a note.

Tell Chief I have volunteer duty at Marshall's school.

I put the SUV into gear and drove toward Cara's. I imagined her in the SUV with me, my hand on her thigh as we drove to dinner. I imagined her leaning over and running her hand up my leg, then whispering something naughty...

"I'm going to suck your dick while you drive. Don't wreck."

I grinned as I pictured her unzipping my pants, freeing my cock, and stroking my shaft with her soft hand.

She leaned down and licked the tip, a drop of pre-come giving her a taste of what was to come. She wrapped her lips around the head and sucked hard, pulling my manhood into her mouth until it hit the back of her throat. I could feel her throat muscles squeeze as she swallowed. Then she pulled back and did it all over again.

"Fuck, baby," I groaned and rubbed my hand over my throbbing erection.

My daydream continued, and I pictured my hand on the back of her head, guiding her down over the length of my cock.

"Fuck yes," I groaned.

She reached her hand into my pants and fondled my balls, giving them a firm squeeze just as she sucked hard on the helmet of my dick.

"I'm going to come, baby," I groaned.

I wanted to pull over and rub this erection out, but I also wanted to hold on to it until I reached Cara's. Just seeing her in person, right now, might cause me to lose my self-control and orgasm on sight.

I sighed, and the daydream continued.

"I wish I could straddle your body and fuck you while you drive," she whispered while she stroked me. *"I need you inside me."*

"I want to be buried balls deep inside you, baby. Soon, very soon."

I stopped at a red light two blocks from Cara's home, and as the crimson hue lit my car, I felt exposed, as if everyone could see the naughtiness of my mind. I cleared my throat and covered my erection with my hand. I needed to calm the fuck down before I got to Cara's, or I would lose my shit.

The light turned green, and I sped through the intersection and turned down her street. After parking, I looked up to the condo unit that was hers and saw her light was on. I smirked. My heart also picked up. Nerves plagued my stomach. The last time I felt something like this, it was for Marshall's mother. I'd been excited to go on a date, to meet new people, to consider something new with someone, but nothing had been like it was with Autumn.

It was time to go inside and talk to my son's teacher, my friend with amazing benefits, the woman who had managed to slip into my heart when I wasn't watching.

♦ ♦ ♦ ♦

Cara opened her door and stood in the frame like an angel, with the light behind her creating an aura around her body. She wore a simple summer dress, yet it was sexy as hell on her. Cara's skin was kissed just enough by the sun to give it a subtle tan. The yellow of the dress was exquisite with her soft pink lips and caramel eyes. Her hair lay braided over her left shoulder. The dress was a halter, and I wanted to untie it and let it fall into a heap on the floor.

God, to have her naked in my arms, her body pressed against mine ... The thought caused my erection to press even harder against my pants.

"Won't you come in?" she asked with a smile. She stepped aside and placed a hand on her hip.

Once in, I turned to face her as she closed the door behind me. As much as I wanted to hold her body up against the door, I needed to keep a bit of distance—at least for now. I wanted to ravage her, but I also needed to know her more. She was, after all, my son's teacher.

"So," she started and held her place by the door for a moment. "You said you wanted to talk?" She made her way toward her kitchen and pulled out two stemmed glasses. "Wine?"

When she looked over to me, I shook my head. "No thank you. I'm more of a beer man."

"You just haven't found the right wine." She turned back to her fridge and pulled out a bottle of white. "Do you like sweet or savory?"

"What does this have to do with wine?"

She grinned and motioned for me to join her in the kitchen. "There's more to wine than just the taste. Do you have a sweet tooth, or are you a meat and potatoes kind of guy?"

"Well, when you put it like that, I would rather have the savory."

She nodded. "Then you'd probably like red wine. Maybe a Merlot. Maybe one night I can take you to a local wine tasting. It'll give you an idea of what you may like and what you'd want to avoid."

I raised my brow. "Do people really swish wine in their mouths and hum through it?"

She giggled. It was cute. When she glanced my way, her nose wrinkled, and her eyes sparkled with mischief. It was adorable, and I wanted to see more of this side of her. "Oh yeah, and they spit it into cups."

I blinked. "Wait, they sip it to taste it and then spit it out?"

She nodded. "Yep."

I'm a man. Of course, my mind went *there*. I pictured Cara on her knees, sucking my cock. And then as I came, she spat it out, as if sampling my come, then thanked me for my time. I chuckled.

"What's so funny?" she asked.

"I don't think you want to know."

She approached with a chilled bottle and handed it to me. "I have an opener in here. Come on. Tell me. I want to know what made you laugh."

With a sigh, I leaned against her counter as she handed me the wine opener. "I thought of you on your knees. Me coming in your mouth, you tasting it and then spitting it out."

Her brows furrowed, and then she giggled. "That is funny!" She shook her head and opened a nearby cabinet. Inside were many bottles of wine. "Ahh, here we go." She pulled out another bottle and turned it toward me.

"This has Marilyn Monroe on it," I said as I took the bottle.

"Yes, it does. It's the 2013 Marilyn Merlot. It's dark and has subtle hints of mocha. It has the right amount of spice, fruitiness from cherries, and a light finish. Go ahead and open it. I bet you'll like it."

"Sure, all right." Like the previous bottle, I used her wine opener.

As the cork came out, she took the bottle and poured a small amount into one of the glasses. She smelled it and then handed it to me. "Go ahead."

She picked up the bottle of white wine, poured herself a glass, and then held it toward me. "Here's to an unusual friendship. One I'm looking forward to exploring further."

I smiled. Her words touched me. It was why I was here. I wanted more, needed more from her. I wasn't one to wham-bam-thank-you-ma'am with someone like Cara. If it was a one-night stand, maybe it would have been different, but this was not that.

"Here's to a beautiful woman who seems to have no bounds." I tilted my wine glass to hers, and they clinked. "And here's to us."

"To us," she repeated and clinked our glasses once more.

I brought the glass to my lips. I wasn't sure what to expect, but I didn't think wine was my thing. I was completely wrong. This Merlot had a soft tang that left no lingering aftertaste. I picked up the hints of mocha she mentioned and the cherries, yet it was almost dry.

"Wow."

She smiled with a nod. "You like it?"

"Absolutely. It's really good. I never would have tried it, but now..."

She held her glass to me once more. "Here's to new experiences."

I tipped and clinked my glass to hers. "Absolutely," I said before taking another sip.

"So, you said you wanted to talk?" She set her glass down.

"Yeah." I took another sip of wine and refilled my glass. I met her gaze, took in a deep breath, and then let it go. "Cara, I like you. A lot. I can't do this friends-with-benefits situation we're in. I thought I could, but honestly, I can't. You're Marshall's teacher. I'll see you more than I thought I would. I don't want your job to be in jeopardy, and hell, I need to focus when I'm on the clock."

I felt a bit dizzy. I'd let all those words out without taking a breath. She didn't speak. I looked to the floor and saw her bare feet, her toenails painted tangerine orange, stepping toward me. She reached for my hands, and my stomach flipped.

"What are you doing?" I whispered.

"I want more, Noah. I don't like this arrangement any more than you do. But . . ."

I held my breath. When there's a *but*, a negative always followed. I lifted my gaze to meet hers.

"I love my job. I can't take a chance of losing what I've worked years to earn. I'll make my tenure this year, but there are a few gunning for my position and a few who wouldn't mind seeing me go."

I frowned. "Some of the teachers want you gone?"

She nodded. "I have parents requesting me personally to teach their young ones. They call me the child whisperer." She chuckled. "If word got out that you and I were an item, I'm concerned I could lose everyone I have in my corner. I'm not saying you're not worth the risk, but I have to think about what's best for me. I'm sure you understand. Would I be worth the risk if it was your job?"

With a sigh, I let go of her hands and crossed my arms over my chest. I didn't quite like where this conversation was going. I wanted to confess how I felt, and here she was, breaking things off with me.

"Well?" She laid her hands on my forearms. "Talk to me."

"What can I say?"

"How about the truth? Tell me what's on your mind."

"The truth?"

She nodded.

"Well, the truth is, I came over tonight in hopes of taking us to the next level. I didn't expect you to break things off."

"Oh, shit." She took a step back. "I'm sorry. Truly. I . . . I'm a dumbass."

I felt my brows furrow as I frowned. "You're not a dumbass,

but why do you feel this way?"

She sighed, picked up her glass of wine, and swallowed the contents. She refilled it and drank it down just as fast.

I poured more of the red wine into my own glass and followed suit.

"Self-preservation," she said.

"What? What the hell does that mean?"

"If I beat you to the punch, then you can't break things off with me."

"You thought... You thought I was breaking it off with you?"

She nodded and covered her face with her hands. "I'm a dumbass."

I chuckled, took her wrists, and then pulled her hands from her face. "You're not a dumbass. In fact, this vulnerability I see in you is exquisite."

She met my gaze, and my God, she had tears in her eyes. Now I felt like the dick. I'd made her cry.

"Cara, I'm sorry. I didn't mean—"

"Shut up," she whispered.

I raised my brows. "What?"

"Shut up and kiss me."

I had wanted to tell her about Marshall's mother, about my feelings, about everything, but with her demand, I was putty in her hands. She was a force to be reckoned with.

I cupped her face, tilted it toward mine, and traced her cheekbones with my thumbs. Her caramel eyes held specs of chocolate, and her pupils widened as she stared into mine.

I leaned in and slanted my lips over hers. She sighed, and I tasted her wine. Our tongues danced through the darkness and light that was savored in our mouths. I wanted this... all of this. I wanted Cara in my life.

I'd had a hole in my heart for many years, and for the first time in a very long time, it started to feel whole again.

I moved my arms around her body and lifted her against me. She wrapped her legs around my waist, and I carried us through the darkness of the hallway to the most familiar room in her home to me. Her bedroom.

Collapsing our bodies onto her bed, I thrust my hips into her, pressing my erection against her pussy.

"I need you," I whispered against her lips. The words hit some part of my inner self. I really did need her. I couldn't let her go. Not now. This whirlwind romance we'd started had taken a drastic turn, and I couldn't wait to see where we would end up.

CHAPTER NINE

CARA

Waking up alone sometimes felt lonely, whereas other days it was liberating. No one to report in to, no one to worry about, no concerns if they were cheating. Then, on the other hand, waking up in love felt as if one had fallen into the deepest pit of euphoria, scented with the person you loved and covering you in a blanket of hope, dreams, and trust.

When I woke this morning, I was alone, but the morning sun awakened me as if I were a flower drinking in the rays. I wanted to jump from my warm bed and dance naked in my room. I wanted to throw my arms in the air and spin until I felt dizzy and fell to my knees.

All of this would be in part because of how I was feeling about Noah. I hadn't wanted Noah in my life. I didn't need him. I wanted nothing to do with him. But the more time we spent together, the more sex we had, the more I saw him outside of my bedroom... I could no longer deny how I felt. I couldn't continue to hold what Jeremy did to me over Noah's head. It wasn't fair to him, and it wasn't fair to me.

With a meow, Luci jumped up onto my bed. I ran my hands through his black fur, the subtle horns on his head pointing skyward.

"Where were you last night when Noah came over?

Hmm? You should meet him, you know? Stop being so shy."

Luci simply purred and rubbed his head against my fingers. I sat up, and my cat jumped to the floor, then ran toward the kitchen. It was breakfast time. How dare I keep my king waiting?

I thought back to last night as I padded into the kitchen. Noah confessing his feelings and me putting up my invisible wall of fortitude. I seldom let anyone in and was a master at keeping everyone out.

But Noah . . . I couldn't quite put my finger on it, but he'd managed to slip past my wall and had barely gained a glimpse of the darkness that was my soul. What would happen when he got to know the real me? Would he run and hide? Or would he stay and fight by my side? My past was like a dragon waiting to be slain, and Noah was the knight to bring the misery to an end.

I pulled a can of cat food from the cabinet, opened it, and placed it on Luci's plate and then took a seat on the barstool in my kitchen. Running my hand through my hair, I felt my stomach flip in pleasant leaps with butterflies reminding me of the giddies Noah brought to my life.

And there was Marshall, his son. Who took care of him when he wasn't at school? Where was he when Noah fought fires or was with me?

I looked to my hands and felt a stab of guilt. I was taking father-and-son time away from Marshall and Noah. Where was his mother? Was Noah divorced? Separated?

Other than the fact that Noah was a firefighter, I didn't really know much else about him. If we were going to do this and take that next step, there were questions I needed answers to. Did Marshall have custody of his son? How involved was his mother? What about grandparents? Information about his mother wasn't in his file at school, so I didn't have much to go on.

With a sigh, I closed my eyes and rubbed my forehead. This was too much to think about on a Saturday morning. I needed coffee. I picked up my phone and pulled up the calendar. There was a date for tonight with Erin and my other girlfriends. We were going to the new bar in town. There was a show tonight, something live with magic or illusions. I couldn't quite remember, but whatever it was, it was perfect timing.

I needed to cool my own personal jets of all things Noah and figure out what I wanted... no, what I *needed* in my life. I had my tenure at the school in the palm of my hands. I was up for a possible promotion and a pay raise. And my parents profited from some stock they sold and wanted to take me on a vacation to Scotland when summer arrived.

I'd always wanted to visit Scotland and see a few men in kilts. Consider it homework for my teaching.

With a smile, I slid off the stool and poured myself a cup of coffee. Then I made my way toward my room. I walked up to my dresser and reached for my drawer, then paused. Noah's T-shirt from our first night together still sat on top of it. I reached for it instead and pulled it to my face. I closed my eyes and inhaled. His familiar scent filled my head. I set the shirt back on the dresser. At some point, I would give the shirt back, but not today, or tomorrow, or anytime soon. For now, it was mine.

◆ ◆ ◆ ◆

The day had settled into the evening, a crisp breeze blew through the Manhattan streets, and the sounds of the city grew louder with every minute that passed. My driver stepped around to my side of the car and opened my door. I thanked him with a tip, then stepped onto the sidewalk. No one drove in Manhattan if they could help it, but it didn't mean one couldn't call for a ride.

I pulled my phone from my purse and texted Erin.

> *Hey, I'm here outside the Starbucks.*
> *Where are you?*

I looked up at the coffee shop in front of me, the line to get in stretching out the door. I shook my head and glanced at my phone when it buzzed.

> *I'm one block away. Be there in a sec.*

I tugged my calf-length cashmere coat around my body and shivered. I checked my phone once more when I heard Erin.

"Hey, I'm here!"

I looked over and found her walking toward me. I smiled and waved to her. "Are you ready to go in?"

She nodded. "It looks like it's just us tonight. The others bailed."

I shrugged. "That's fine." I took a step back and looked at her attire. She wore a long black coat, similar to mine, and underneath it, she had on a one-piece jumpsuit with no sleeves or shoulders. It was still fall, but it felt more like winter tonight. She would freeze.

"And where's the rest of your wardrobe?" I asked.

She laughed. "Funny. I happen to look hot in this."

"Yeah, maybe so, but it's cold tonight."

Without another word on her wardrobe choice, we walked toward our destination. The new club was two blocks down from the Starbucks, and I was looking forward to something different, something new, something that wasn't Noah.

"So," Erin started and slipped her hand through my arm. "Who's the guy?"

I frowned and looked over to her. "I don't know what you mean."

"Don't play like that. You're glowing like the cat who ate the fucking canary. Now come on. Who is it? Spill. I need details."

I didn't want to tell her anything about Noah. Wait, she'd said I was glowing. "You think I'm glowing, like I'm in love or something?"

"Totally. Now tell me, please. I have zero life right now except for my TV remote and my BOB."

I snickered. I could relate to being single and having a BOB. BOB never talked back or told you where to go or who to go with. He only turned on and off and occasionally needed a change of batteries. Best boyfriend ever.

"There is no one, Erin." The conversation I had with her about Noah came to mind. I couldn't tell her I was seeing him. At least not yet. I doubt she'd understand or agree with it. It wasn't exactly professional to date your student's parent.

But then again, were we dating? After last night's conversation, I suppose that would be a yes.

"Hello? Earth to Cara. Where did you go just now?"

"What?" I asked her. "I didn't go anywhere. I'm right here, and look, here's the club. Let's go in and talk about our love lives later, okay?"

"Sure. But you can't fool me. I know something's up."

I was relieved she let it go, but her last words had me wondering just how much she really knew. Either way, I bet she would continue to hound me until I gave every last detail about who Mr. Right Now was.

The club was dark, lit only by the thin tall letters atop of the entrance. There was a line of people waiting to get in. I took note of the bouncer and security guard at the door.

"Stay by my side, okay?" I told Erin.

"You got it." She held on to my arm a little tighter as we made our approach.

My mother told me long ago that to get anywhere in the world, you needed a good purse, great shoes, and at least a hundred dollars in your hand at any given moment.

Well, right now was that moment, and taking no was not an option.

We approached the two men, and I felt like a midget next to their stature. One looked over his sunglasses, which was odd since it was night. The other glared at me, Erin, then back to me.

"Name?" he growled.

"Cara Murphy," I told him. I held a piece of white paper in my hand that was wrapped around a Ben Franklin.

He snatched the paper from my hand and opened it. He looked at me once more, then marked something on his clipboard. He motioned for us to go inside with a move of his head.

"Thank you," I told him.

"Thank you," Erin repeated.

"You're welcome. Anything you ladies need, just call Tony."

"Are you Tony?" I asked.

He nodded. "Yes, ma'am. Enjoy your night."

I smiled. "Thank you, Tony. Don't work too hard."

He chuckled, and we stepped inside. The cold of the breeze was replaced by a chilled room. The walls were lit by blue lights that shined against newly tiled walls. Steps led us down toward a bar on the right and couches on the left, with a hardwood dance floor between them. Above us hung a large orb of white lights with a red hue shining from the inside. At the other end of the room was a stage with props and equipment for the show tonight.

Jazz music played, and I pointed to a flight of stairs that led to balcony seats. She nodded, and we headed up. Moments after we took a seat, a waitress took our drink order.

We removed our jackets, and a man in a tuxedo stopped by our table.

"May I hang your jackets, ladies?"

Next to our tables were coat hangers. I nodded and handed my coat over to him. Our waitress returned with our drinks, and the music grew louder. More people came in, and on the stage, the entertainment began to set up.

"Any idea what we're in for tonight?" Erin asked.

I shook my head. "I don't really know, but by the looks of it, they almost seem to be circus performers." I pointed to a set of long sticks that had round ends, almost like giant matches.

"Is that a torch?" Erin asked.

I followed her finger to where she pointed, and sure enough, there was a torch with the equipment. "Great, they're playing with fire."

"Maybe the fire department will pay another visit," Erin teased.

I looked at Erin and raised my brow. "Oh yeah, maybe."

Soon, the club filled with people, and the entertainment for the evening was ready to kick off.

The man on stage picked up the microphone. "So... I asked the club tonight to turn off the fire sprinklers."

He didn't get a response, and I glanced to Erin. I leaned over to her. "I hope he's kidding."

"Right, okay, so we're getting started now. Enjoy! We're Pyros at Night!"

I sighed and shook my head. "A fire show in a new club. What could go wrong?" I took a sip of my drink and heard Erin laughing. I turned to her and found her talking to a random man who took a seat next to her. Erin was beautiful, and the outfit she wore would attract a lot of attention.

Point made. *Well played, Erin.*

I picked up my drink to take another sip when the man on the stage lit one of the sticks. He began tossing it about and actually dropped one of them. I raised my brow and watched him bend over to grab it then leap up.

"I meant to do that," he yelled into the microphone.

I glanced over to the entrance and found people were leaving as quickly as they were trying to get in.

New club.

Bad first night show.

Not a good sign for the establishment.

I sure hoped they had insurance.

"Listen," I said and leaned over to Erin. "I'm going to finish my drink and go. This show tonight isn't my scene."

When she didn't say anything, I tapped her shoulder.

She turned with a frown. "What?"

I raised my brows. "Well, okay, then. Enjoy your night." I

stood and finished my drink.

"Don't go," she said and reached for my hand.

"No, it's all right. Enjoy your night and have fun"—I motioned to the guy she was talking to—"I'm bored with Pyro and his fire."

"Do you want me to go with you?" she asked.

I shook my head and reached for my jacket. As I pulled it from the hook, I heard a few screams. I immediately looked to the stage and saw the pyro guy had caught one of the curtains behind him on fire and then his pants as well.

"Fucking perfect," I groaned.

A second later, a loud alarm sounded, and the emergency storm lights automatically switched on all over the club. Then the fire sprinklers kicked in.

I growled and headed toward the door. I'd just had my jacket returned from the cleaners. Thankfully, a little water wouldn't ruin it. The people attempting to head down the stairs came to a stop. Those trying to flee were jamming the entrance door. I sighed and leaned against the stair rail. No one was getting in or out, and soon the fire department would be here.

Holy hell, would Noah be part of the crew?

With a sigh, I lowered my eyes to my phone in my hand. I was tempted to text him to come and get me. But it was Manhattan. Only way he would get through would be on a fire engine.

I had never felt this helpless in my entire life. I was thrust into a situation like Rapunzel, waiting on my tower of stairs, blocked from the exit. My fireman knight would rush in with his fire hose and put out the flames, then carry me away in his arms.

Then again, I wasn't much of a fairy tale kind of woman. I wasn't the damsel needing a rescue. I was the knight in this tale and would save myself.

Suddenly a gap formed and people began to leave the club. I made my way down the stairs and pulled up the Uber app. I requested a ride and hoped they would be here by the time I made my way outside.

As soon as I made it to the door, red lights were flashing against the walls of the buildings. The sirens wailed as they came down the street. Cars pulled to the sides to allow the engines through. I could see the firefighters on the trucks equipped with their turnout gear, and I looked for Noah, hoping to catch a glimpse of my firefighter.

Just as I made my way to the exit, the men and women in uniform came rushing forward. Two with a hose, three with extinguishers.

I didn't see Noah in any of their faces. A part of me felt relieved, the other disappointed.

I tightened my jacket and checked my phone. My ride was a few blocks away. I stood on the sidewalk and glanced around for Erin but couldn't see or hear her. She was lost in the crowd, probably with her new guy of the night. She could take care of herself. If there was trouble, she had my number.

I checked my phone again, and my driver was coming up the road.

"Finally," I whispered.

"Cara?"

My eyes widened, and my heart jumped into my throat. I glanced over my shoulder, and there was Noah in his firefighter jacket and pants, a helmet on his head.

"Hi," I said and folded my arms in front of me. I was

positive I looked like a drenched cat. I pushed my hair from my face, the wetness of it sending a shiver through my body.

"Are you all right? Do you need medical attention? Were you hurt?"

I shook my head. "No, I'm absolutely fine. Only wet as hell. The performer didn't fare so well, though."

"The fire is pretty much out," he said and took a step toward me. "Do you have a ride home?"

"Why? Would you let me ride your engine?"

He chuckled and grinned that Cheshire grin I'd come to enjoy. "If you like, I'll be happy to let you ride my engine."

I pressed my lips together, then shook my head. "I'll take a rain check on that." I looked to my phone and saw my ride was here. "I need to go. I'll call you later?"

He nodded. "Hey, I'm off in a few hours. I can come back if you want?"

"No, she's fine. In fact, she's with me." Erin came up to my side and laced her arm around mine. "Go put out your fire, Mr. Hughes. I'll get my girl here home."

I pulled my arm away. Anger shot through me like gasoline poured on an open flame. "Don't do that."

"Don't do what? Protect you?" she argued.

"Protect me from what? Go home, Erin."

I made my way to my ride and looked back to Noah. He held his hand up like a phone and mouthed *Call me.*

I looked to the driver.

"You called for an Uber?" the driver said.

I looked at him, then his profile on my phone. "Yes, thank you for coming. Bad night."

"Yeah, I can see that," he said as he put the car into gear.

I slid into the back seat and glanced back to Erin. She was

saying something to Noah and then patted him on the chest and walked past him. He looked over to me as we were pulling away.

I pulled his name up on my phone and sent him a text.

> *Come over when you're done. You can*
> *shower at my place.*

I pressed Send. I didn't expect a return text until much later.

Tonight did not go as expected. Hell, it was horrible. However, with the coming visit of Noah, it was about to get a lot better.

And I could hardly wait.

CHAPTER TEN

NOAH

Three hours before my shift ended, there was a club fire. I expected to arrive and get right to work putting out the fire as quickly as possible. What I didn't count on was seeing Cara Murphy at the location. She was soaked from the sprinklers. She stood before me like a lost deer hoping to sneak away from the predator before she was found. However, this predator wanted to pounce her into submission.

Her hair stuck to the arms of her jacket and her face. When she went to move it from her eyes, her jacket opened enough to see the dress she wore. It was black and fitted. At least I think it was, but then again, she was wet. And holy hell, her nipples were fully erect and begging for my mouth.

If it weren't for the public setting, the cold in the air, and my fire suit, I'd consider taking her right here in my fire engine. That would be my fantasy with Cara, taking her at the station in the engine.

She mentioned a shower at her place? Hell, yes. I needed to let Mom know I wouldn't be home to get Marshall until later in the morning.

"Nice seeing you, Noah," Erin said and patted my chest as she passed by. "Whatever you're doing with Cara, you should end it."

I blinked at Erin's words. "Wow…" I shook my head in disbelief. I wonder if Cara knew her friend thought of her this way. Relationship material or not, what I had with Cara is none of Erin's business.

Erin turned to respond, but I didn't give her a chance. I ran past her and headed back toward my crew.

Pushing the conversation aside for a moment, I headed inside the building. The fire was out, and nothing else needed tending. The man I assumed to be the owner was on the phone yelling, then turning to another man and screaming profanities about being an idiot.

Well, who hired who here?

"At what point did we stop playing with matches?" one of my fighter buddies asked.

I shrugged. "Apparently some of us never grow out of it."

"Who was the woman?" he asked.

I smiled and thought of Cara. Was she my girlfriend or just a friend I was fucking? Definite friend, but more than fucking. "She's someone I'm seeing," I decided on.

"Well, she's hot, even when she's wet. Nice one."

I chuckled. "Thanks. All right, the police are here now. Let's wrap up and head back."

The chief came over and handed me a long stick burned black. "Seems our pyromaniac was setting up for a flame show. New paint inside plus non-fire-resistant clothes equal serious party foul."

I shook my head. It could have been much worse than it was. The entire place could have gone up in flames, with Cara inside. I climbed into the engine and removed my helmet. It was cold outside, but I was hot and sweaty. I ran my fingers through my damp hair, and soot beaded on my hand.

Great. Blond hair with black streaks. A shower would definitely be in my future.

At Cara's.

I grinned and leaned back against the engine wall, then closed my eyes. Chatter from the others drowned away as I relaxed and recalled the image of her standing on the sidewalk. She was soaked, cold, beautiful, and her nipples were begging for a suckle.

With a groan and a sigh, I adjusted myself in my turnout gear. I felt the engine kick forward as we pulled away from the nightclub.

◆ ◆ ◆ ◆

Almost three hours had passed between seeing Cara at the nightclub and when I arrived at her condo building. I stepped inside and made my way up the stairs. Two flights up, her view looked out over the park. Not that I'd seen it. I had only been here in the evenings. Maybe one day I'd be able to wake up by her side and enjoy a morning with her.

When I reached her door, I knocked and then waited. A shadow fell over the peephole, and I heard the locks release. She pulled the door back and stood in the frame like an angel.

She wore a white satin nightgown with a matching robe. Her hair was still wet, probably freshly washed, and braided over her shoulder.

"Hello," she said with a smile.

"Hi." I stepped forward.

She took a step back and closed the door behind me. She smiled and locked the door. "You're still covered in sweat and soot."

I took a step closer and touched her chin. Lifting it just enough to lean in, I pressed my lips across hers. "You invited me to clean up here. I was not going to pass up that opportunity."

She giggled. "Come on. I'll show you the way." She took my hand and led me through her home. I knew the way, but I let her lead regardless. We made our way through her bedroom, somewhere I had become intimately familiar with. The bed was made, and a spot was disheveled as if she were sitting on it and scooted off.

She flipped on the light to the bathroom, then turned to face me. "Here we are. Take all the time you need." Cara turned her back to me and opened the shower door.

I moved closer to her, close enough for my chest to graze her back. When I moved my hands over her waist, she let go of the faucet and leaned back against me. I moved my hands up the slick material of her gown to her breasts. Her nipples pressed into my palms. I squeezed the generous mounds, and she gasped a soft whimper.

She reached up and slipped a hand around my neck. Her other hand settled over mine against her breast. I looked down and widened my eyes at the mess I'd made of her gown.

"Shit," I whispered. "Your nightgown . . ."

"Don't worry about it. Nothing I can't get washed."

My breath came out in a rush against her neck and earlobe. The bathroom began to steam with the heat of the water. I welcomed it, relished it.

"Shower with me," I whispered against her ear, then nibbled on the lobe.

A moan escaped her lips, soft and feminine. "Okay," she answered.

I slipped the robe from her body, then slid the spaghetti

straps of her gown down her arms. The fabric fell in a heap to the floor. Cara stood naked before me, my beautiful angel. She turned to face me. Her hair still braided, she removed the holder and began to unbraid it.

I reached for her hair and began to undo her braid for her. Settling her locks behind her back, I ran my fingers through it, then with a gentle yank, I tugged her head back.

She gasped as my mouth slanted against hers. She tugged at my shirt and pushed it up my body. I broke from the kiss just long enough for her to toss my shirt. She fiddled with my pants, then growled against my lips.

"That was so hot," I told her. "Growl for me again, baby."

"Your damn pants. I can't get them undone. Get them off. Shower now. Naked. Come on." She stepped into the shower and motioned for me to join her.

I chuckled and quickly stripped. I kicked my pants, shoes, and socks to the side and stepped under the hot water.

She closed the door and reached up for my hair. She moved her fingers through it as the water ran over my head. I felt her lips feather across my chest as my body became drenched.

"Cara," I whispered her name.

She met my gaze, and it was then that I realized she had no makeup on. She was a natural beauty. Her skin blushed from the heat of the water; maybe it was the heat of our bodies as well.

"Yes?"

"I need you," I told her. Every ounce of me knew this was the truth. I needed her. More than a friend. More than a fuck. I wanted her in my life.

"You have me." She reached for the shampoo and poured it into her hands. "On your knees. Let me wash you."

I raised my brows.

"Come on," she pleaded. "Let me do this for you."

I did not defy her. I wanted to please her just to see her smile. I lowered myself to my knees and looked up to the alluring enchantress before me. She had me under her spell, and I had no intentions of leaving.

She moved her hands through my hair, scrubbing my scalp. It was an amazing feeling, something I had taken for granted. I would ask for this again in the future. When she rinsed me clean, she stood over me, her lips set in a smirk.

I took the opportunity to soak in her body. I wanted to memorize every inch of her, taste every part of her. I reached for her hips, pulled her closer, and pressed my lips to her navel.

She giggled, and I felt her stomach flinch. "That tickles," she said in a soft voice.

I smirked and looked up at her. I stood to my feet and reached for her soap. I gave my body a good wash. When I set the soap down, I motioned for her to come closer. When she did, I moved my fingers through her wet locks and cradled her head. "I want to be inside you, and as much as I want to fuck you here in the shower, I'd rather take you to your bed and make love to you."

I felt her body give way with a sigh under my hold, and I wrapped my other arm around her. I smirked, teasing her lips with my tongue. With my gentle licks against her upper lip, she gave way and swiped her tongue across mine. I tightened the grip in her hair and claimed her lips.

She wrapped her arms around my neck and held on.

"The water," I mumbled against her lips. She reached around me and turned it off. Immediately my body chilled from the loss of the heat.

"Come on," she whispered and pulled herself free from my grip. She wrapped herself in a towel and handed one to me. I dried myself enough to get the water from my body, then hung it. I didn't give her a chance to finish.

Grabbing Cara by her waist, I turned her around, and she squealed. I bent down, pulled her to my shoulder, and lifted her into the air.

"Oh my God, you caveman!" She laughed and slapped an open hand across my bare ass.

"Hey, that stung!" I chuckled and laid a smack across her derrière.

She squealed once more, and I let her fall onto her bed. She bounced once, then scooted back to her headboard.

I lifted my brows and rolled my shoulders. I leaned onto the bed and began to crawl toward her. She grinned and moved one of her feet toward my hand, and I grabbed her ankle and pulled her toward me.

"Noah!" she screamed with laughter.

The bed cover and sheets pulled down as I dragged her, and I chuckled. I pressed a knee between her legs, and she opened for me. Looking down at her pussy, bare and glistening, I knew she was ready for me. I met her gaze and paused.

"I don't have a condom with me."

"I'm on the pill," she answered.

I grinned and leaned down to her. I pressed my lips to hers and teased her pussy with my dick.

"Please," she begged. "Please, fuck me. I need you."

"Cara," I whispered in a heavy breath. I wanted to push inside her, feel everything there was about Cara wrap around my cock as it filled her. "Are you sure? No condom?"

"Yes," she told me and lifted her legs around my waist. "I

want you with no condom inside me. I want to feel you."

I groaned, and my balls pulsed. I had only touched her on the surface and was ready to explode. I reached between us and grabbed my dick, pressed it against her, then pushed.

I pulled back and thrust back inside her. Cara held on to my shoulders, and her back arched underneath me. With every push, she moaned. She was this perfect woman who held nothing back. She wanted me as much as I wanted her.

Her walls clamped around my cock and squeezed, her honey coating me. I needed more of her. I was consumed by her.

I pushed myself back on my heels, grabbed her legs, and pulled her up to my waist. I held her by the hips and began to thrust hard and fast into her pussy. Our bodies slapped in the silence of her room. Beads of sweat formed on my brow as well as on her chest and stomach.

I still needed more. "Come here, baby girl," I growled.

She met my gaze, and without a whisper, she knew exactly what I wanted. Cara sat up and straddled my body. I moved to sit with my legs stretched out front. She rocked against my cock, taking me deeper with each move she made. As she rolled, I thrust upward. We moved in a beautiful union.

"Cara," I groaned. "Damn, woman, I'm going to come very soon."

She placed her hands on the sides of my face and rested her forehead to mine. "Come with me," she whispered.

I gripped the back of her thighs and held her against me. She was my match in every way possible. An emptiness inside me filled in this moment, and for me, there was no going back.

"Cara!"

A warm rush of heat soaked my cock as she came. She

tilted her head back and groaned out loud into the bedroom just as my balls tightened. I lost myself in her tonight, and I never wanted to be found.

Our breathing slowed, and Cara lowered her gaze to mine. No words were exchanged. None were needed. She slipped her arm around my neck and pulled herself close.

And I held on to this woman who had found her way into my life by a chance meeting, and fate had brought us together once more as my son's teacher.

I'd never been one to believe in or leave anything to fate, but after meeting Cara, all of that had completely changed.

And I'd fallen in love with her.

CHAPTER ELEVEN

CARA

The moment you begin to wake from a dream of perfection, the one you want to remain in because it was complete ecstasy . . . The moment you're running through a field and your body soars, when the man you've wanted for so long confesses you're the one for him, or the moment you're making love in a dream and the most intense orgasm of your life begins . . . and then your eyes open the hell up.

I groaned and turned on my side. Reaching to my clit, I rub my fingers vigorously in hopes of capturing the last essence of the climax that teased at the surface of my consciousness. The hardened bundle of nerves pulsed as if to mock my attempt. The sensation disappeared as quickly as it came.

A different type of groan—one of frustration—escaped this time. With a sigh, I relaxed my arms and longed for sleep to pull me back under. It was Sunday, and I had nowhere to be.

Then I felt my bed move, and fear raced up my spine. No one was here with me, were they?

Last night came back in a flash.

The nightclub.

The fire.

Noah.

I opened my eyes and stared at my ceiling. I was on the

right side of the bed. Normally, I would be right in the middle with a fortress of pillows. Not this morning, though.

Was Noah in my bed asleep? Did he stay the night? We had sex… No, we had made the most incredible love last night. It went much deeper than any previous time I was with him. Hell, it was more than I ever experienced with Jeremy. Noah touched a part of my soul.

Closing my eyes, I took in a deep breath, then turned my head toward the left side of my bed. When I opened them once more, there was Noah, sound asleep. His body was turned to face mine. His face was gentle and soft. A shadow of a beard touched his cheeks, lips, and chin. His eyes danced side to side behind his lids. What was he dreaming about? Me? Fighting fires?

I don't remember the last time I had a man sleep over. In fact, we hadn't discussed him staying. We must have fallen asleep after sex. It was late. He had worked a long shift, and then there was the nightclub fire.

Curiosity grew as I stared at the man in my bed. What would it be like to wake up next to him every morning? Or be by his side every night? Would he even want to take what we had that far and choose to stay with me? What about Marshall? What about my teaching?

Everything would find its rightful place in due time. Right now it was figuring out what this was between us and if this was what I wanted. I liked Noah. I really liked him. I could see myself with him, side by side. Grocery shopping, the movies, holiday events.

But I never considered myself a parent. Did I want children? Sure, one day, but taking on the role of stepmother wasn't high on my agenda. I loved teaching kids, but having to deal with someone's ex was not in my plans. Marshall was a great kid, but being his teacher *and* his dad's girlfriend was a lot for me to take in.

"Are you watching me sleep?"

I smiled at the groggy sound of Noah's voice. It was sexy and something I wouldn't mind hearing again. "Maybe. I didn't realize you stayed the night."

"I didn't realize I fell asleep in your bed. I hope it's okay?" He opened his eyes, and his baby blues met my gaze.

Noah was not asking me for more than I was willing to give him. Staying over was not a deal breaker. In fact, I wouldn't mind him staying over more.

I nodded. "Yes, of course."

Noah opened his arms and waited. He motioned with his fingers for me to envelop his body. More than anything, I wanted this. Oh God did I want this, but in doing so, I was letting one of my walls down. I would be letting Noah in.

With great risk comes great reward. Perfect sentiment.

I was risking another heartbreak by allowing myself to open up to Noah. Right now, it was a risk I was willing to take. I smiled and scooted across the bed, into his waiting arms. This awoke a part of my soul that had been asleep for far too long. It was a hole that had been waiting to be filled, and Noah had filled it.

I settled my cheek to his chest, then slipped my arm around his waist. His pecs had a tuft of hair just between them, but the rest of his body was smooth. His body was firm and strong, delectable and mouthwatering. We'd just woken, but I wanted to taste him.

But that would need to wait. Right now, I simply wanted to just be. I let out a long sigh and felt my body relax into his, a perfect fit, as if we were molded for each other.

Noah began to play with a few strands of my hair. Silence passed between us for a long moment before he spoke.

"I want to talk to you about Marshall and his mother."

I opened my eyes. This was not just a conversation about people. This was "the talk."

"Okay," I whispered.

"I want you in my life, Cara. I want you in Marshall's. You need to know what happened to her."

My throat dried, and I had a hard time swallowing. I needed water, but I didn't want to move. "Only if you want to tell me," I managed to get out.

I felt Noah's chest move to inhale and slowly let the air go. This had to be as hard on him as it was for me. I had a past as well that I wanted to share with Noah.

"Let me go first," I blurted out before I realized what I had said.

"What?" he asked.

I closed my eyes and gritted my teeth. *What the hell, Murphy?*

"Yeah, I need to go first," I insisted.

"All right," Noah said. "Go ahead."

I pulled out of his arms and brought my left arm under my head. He did the same on his right side.

"When I moved out here to New York, it wasn't for a job or chasing a dream. I did it for a guy. Jeremy." Other than a few of my close friends I'd made in my few years in Manhattan, I hadn't filled anyone else in on the crap I went through with my ex. "I followed him out here when he accepted a job offer. I'd always wanted to visit New York, and it was a great opportunity for me. I thought I would teach, and we'd get married and start a family. We'd come home after a long day and tell each other everything that happened. Well, one day, I found him fucking someone in our bed. It . . . it broke me. It shattered my soul. I swore off men. I swore I would never allow anyone to get that close to me again." I lowered my eyes to the bed and fiddled with the pillowcase. "Then I met you."

Noah brushed my hair behind my ear.

I raised my eyes and met his stare. "You've managed to piece my soul back together again. I never even saw you coming."

A genuine smile spread across his lips. His eyes glistened with unshed tears. "I am very glad to hear you say that." He ran his fingers across my cheek. "Where are you originally from?"

"I was born and raised in Sumner County, Tennessee. Just south of Kentucky."

He raised his brows. "Wow, my own little country girl."

I laughed and shook my head. "No country girl here. That might be my roots, but I've become a bona fide city girl here in Manhattan."

It felt amazing to share my past with this man, my man. Was he mine? After last night, waking up in my bed, and now sharing personal information? Yes, he was indeed my boyfriend. My stomach did a little flip of excitement from this knowledge.

"Thank you for sharing your story. Jeremy's loss. He had no idea what a catch you are."

"Damn straight."

He smirked and leaned in. Noah pressed his lips to my forehead, then hesitated.

"What is it?" I asked. Was he scared to share about his ex? He was with me, so I was of course assuming she was his ex.

JULIE MORGAN

This was the mother of his child. I could never compete with that. It was an expectation I could never step up to.

Unless we had children.

Nope, not right now.

"I was married to Marshall's mother for four years before she became pregnant with him. Her name was Autumn. All she wanted in life was to be a mother. She wanted to stay home with him while I worked and supported our family. We were happy."

It did not get past me that he referred to Autumn in past tense.

"Then, just before she was going to give birth to Marshall, she became sick. I rushed her to the hospital, but by the time they realized what was happening, it was too late."

"Oh, Noah," I whispered and took his hand. I gave it a gentle squeeze.

"She had complained of headaches and body aches, but she figured it was the pregnancy. Her white blood cell count would have been high with the pregnancy, and the doctors had no reason to test her for it at the time. When I took her in toward the end of her pregnancy, it was then they realized she had bone cancer."

He fell silent, and a single tear slid down his cheek.

I touched his face with my palm and swiped the tear with my thumb. "I'm so sorry," I whispered.

"She gave birth to Marshall and held him in her arms. A few hours later, her body couldn't hold on, and she passed away."

"Oh, Noah," I whispered and pulled him into my arms. Now it was me he needed, my arms, my strength. I felt a dampness on my skin, and I knew it was his tears. The painful memory of his wife's passing was relived in this moment he shared with me.

And Marshall never knew his mother. It was a tragedy no one should ever experience.

"Noah, I'm so very sorry. I wish I could have met her if circumstances were different."

He nodded then sniffed. He lifted his head from my chest and wiped his face with a quick swipe. "You would have liked her. In a way, you remind me of her."

"Oh yeah?"

He nodded. "Your personality. You two would have been good friends." He chuckled, then let a long sigh go. "I haven't been in a relationship with anyone since she passed. Marshall has been my whole world. My mom has helped in raising him. Autumn's parents moved away a few years ago. They wanted time to heal from their daughter's death. I haven't heard much from them, but they send Marshall holiday and birthday cards."

I remained quiet while listening and kept my opinion about the grandparents leaving to myself. I didn't agree with the grandparents moving away, but it was their choice to go. "I'm happy to hear about your mom being here for you."

"She's been amazing through all of this with me. No one expected Autumn to pass away. The only one not affected by it is Marshall. He didn't know her, so how could he miss her?"

"Well, Marshall is an incredible kid." And he truly was. He was kind to the other students in class and was genuinely a happy child.

"Would you like to meet my mom one day?"

My brows rose. I wasn't expecting the parent question, but with everything we've shared, it made sense.

"Oh, I'm sorry. Too soon?" he asked.

I smiled and shook my head. "No, not too soon. I'd love to meet her. But if it's okay to ask, what happened to your father?"

He nodded. "It's fine to ask. He passed away a decade ago."

"Oh, I'm sorry to hear that. My father also passed away. He's not been gone for a long time, but it has become easier. It's been my mom and me for a while. He had a heart attack."

"That had to be hard on you."

I nodded and looked at my hands. "I wish I knew what to say about Autumn."

"There's nothing to say."

I looked at him, and he offered an encouraging smile. His eyes lit up with hope, as if a new day would grant an escape from the pain. "My mom found a great support group and was able to get through it. She's doing just fine."

"That's good to hear," I said. "Well, if we're going to do the family sharing, maybe first we should sit down and talk to Marshall?"

He smiled and laid his head back on the pillow next to me. "Yeah, I guess we should. But what do I say? 'Hey, little man. Guess what? Your teacher is my girlfriend.'"

I grinned, and when Noah met my gaze, he chuckled.

"What's the smile about?" he asked. "You look like the kid who was given free access to the cookie jar."

I shrugged my right shoulder. "You called me your girlfriend."

He returned my smile. "So I did." Noah then reached for me and pulled me on top of him. It was so fast, I squealed, then laughed. He lifted up and met my lips with a kiss.

"Cara Murphy, you're an amazing woman. And I have fallen in love with you."

I smiled even bigger this time. I'd thought I'd loved

Jeremy, but I'd been more in love with the idea of being in love. However, with Noah, it was different. This was life-changing, scream-from-the-rooftops-for-everyone-to-hear love.

"I've been waiting my entire life for you, Noah Hughes, and I never realized it until we met. You've managed to break down all of my walls and fill a damaged hole in my heart. I am unconditionally and irrevocably in love with you."

Noah sat us up and hugged my body to his. This was the second time anyone had ever held me this way. Last night was the first time.

I wanted my forever with my firefighter.

But how would I manage this with my career at school and Marshall being my student?

CHAPTER TWELVE

NOAH

That feeling when everything fell into place and you found yourself wondering, looking, waiting for the other shoe to drop. You knew it was too good to be true. The quickened heartbeat of finding love, the flips of the stomach when you thought of the person. Finding yourself searching for air to breathe because someone completely took your breath away.

It was how I felt about Cara. I hadn't felt this since Autumn, and to be honest, the feeling frightened me. It was like approaching a burning building. I knew what to do and how to do it, but I suddenly found myself questioning everything I'd ever known.

It was a familiar situation, but everything about it scared me to death. Would I run inside to put out the fire like the hero I knew I was, or would I run and hide? I wasn't a fucking coward, but this situation with Cara had me beyond scared. She claimed she was in love with me, but I couldn't help the feeling of insecurity.

I was afraid she'd want to cut and run. I couldn't fathom trying to recover from another broken heart, and I understood why she wouldn't let her guard down to anyone. Walking in on your significant other cheating? That was a pain I'd never experienced. At the same time, Cara had never lost a lover the way I had lost Autumn.

Cara and I were two broken, lost souls looking to heal and find ourselves. And if I was fortunate enough to call her mine, she just might be the missing piece to make me whole again.

I stood in the center of my parents' home and stared at the framed portraits on the wall. Pictures of me from kindergarten through high school hung in order—six on top, seven below. Then the portrait of when I graduated college with my forestry degree. I had graduated a few years before Marshall was born, and at one point, I had wanted to work in agriculture and maybe further my education in environmental science. However, when Autumn died, my college aspirations died with her.

Toward the end of the wall hung a framed poem my mother printed a few years ago. She enjoyed Robert Frost and had a few of his works on her bookshelves. I moved closer to the frame and read the words to his famous poem, "Fire and Ice."

The purpose of the words didn't make sense to me when I first read it, but with the loss of my wife and now finding Cara, the words rang clear.

My eyes burned with the threat of tears. Taking in a deep breath, I turned around and found my mother watching me.

"How long have you been standing there?"

She smiled and took a few steps forward. Time had been kind to her over the years. Her emerald eyes had laugh lines around them, and the same type of lines pulled the corners of her lips in a smile. Her hair hung to her shoulders and was a beautiful silver.

"Long enough," she said. "What's on your mind?"

I sighed. "Everything and nothing. I don't even know where to begin."

"How about starting from the beginning? Come on, I'll make you some tea."

I shook my head. "No time. I need to get Marshall home and in bed."

She held her hand up and waved me off. "Not tonight, son. He's been bathed and is already in bed. I read him a story, and he fell asleep shortly after. And there's a bed already made up for you. So follow me to the kitchen and tell me what's going on. I haven't seen you this . . . hell, I don't even know what to call this."

I chuckled. "Fine, Mother. You win." I yawned and didn't want to argue. I was tired and wanted to be somewhere safe. Not that Cara's or my home wasn't safe, but here with my mom, I could be me. Sometimes I just needed to let all the stress and anxiety of the world go. This was a sanctuary for me, and I needed it more than I'd realized.

We made our way to the kitchen. The walls were wallpapered in a light yellow with soft sea-green leaves painted in a vertical stripe pattern. This was the same wallpaper I grew up with. I often offered to change it out for her, but she enjoyed it still.

She filled two coffee mugs from the filtered water in her fridge, then put them in the microwave. She leaned against the counter and raised her brows. When I didn't start to talk, she motioned with her hand as if to suggest I "continue."

I sighed and lowered myself into one of the chairs at the dining room table and then slouched back.

"I met someone." I looked up to meet her gaze.

She was smiling. "And?"

I shrugged. "I don't know how I feel about it."

"You don't know how you feel about her or the situation?"

"Her? The situation? Both? Yeah . . . both." I ran my hand through my hair and groaned. "And the guilt is eating my gut like it's at an all-you-can-eat buffet."

She raised her brows and chuckled. "Well, that's a horrible description, son. Is it making you feel sick or something?"

"Yeah," I said and stood when the microwave beeped. She pulled out both mugs and set them on the counter. She grabbed chamomile tea, and I picked an English breakfast one. We steeped our tea in silence while my stomach churned from the admission of my feelings.

"The guilt is more than I thought I could handle. I can't eat, sleep, or function. I don't want it to interfere with my job, but I also want to see more of her. And to be honest, Mom, she scares the hell out of me."

She opened the fridge and pulled the heavy cream out for me. I put some in my tea and stirred it. When she put the creamer back, she turned to me and placed a hand on my shoulder.

"You know it's okay to be happy. You're allowed to move on and find happiness with someone else."

I put my hand over hers for a moment, then made my way back to the table and took a seat. My mother sat next to me. I stared at my tea and watched the swirls of the creamer as it settled.

"How did you meet?"

"Don't judge me," I grumbled under my breath.

She let a soft laugh go, then squeezed my hand. "Safe place, remember?"

I nodded and met her gaze. "I went to a club one night with some of my friends from work. That's where we met."

"Okay, so you've seen her more than this one time, I gather?"

I nodded. "Yes, quite a few times. She has this amazing personality. She doesn't let anything get to her and just rolls with the punches."

"What's her name, son?"

"Cara." I felt myself smile at the mention of her name. My belly warmed with the memory of her, and my heart sped at the thought of her in my arms.

"Well, I can see she means a lot to you. Tell me more about this Cara?"

"It's complicated."

"No, son, love isn't complicated. It is or it isn't. There's no gray area in between how people feel."

I took a sip of my tea, then set it down. I palmed my forehead in my hand and let another sigh escape. "No, it's complicated for a different reason." I turned my head just enough to look into her eyes. "On the first day of school, when I took Marshall to meet his teacher?" She nodded, and I continued. "Miss Murphy, Marshall's teacher, is Cara."

Her eyes widened. "And you had no idea?"

I sat back in my chair and crossed my arms over my chest. "No fucking idea."

"Noah, language."

A laugh pushed from my lips like an exhale. "Sorry, Mom. But no, I had no idea."

"So is this what complicates it?"

I nodded. "I don't want to compromise her job by seeing me."

"Has she said as much?"

I nodded. "But she's in this as much as I am."

"Then what's the problem, son?"

I lay my head back against the chair and let out another

exasperated sigh. "I feel as if I'm cheating on Autumn's memory and the life we had."

I closed my eyes, and it felt like a good five minutes of silence passed between us. Curious, I brought my head back up and looked to my mother.

"Do you want me to tell you that you're cheating on your dead wife?"

I frowned. Was that what I wanted? I had no idea. A part of me wanted the ground to open and swallow me whole. Another part wanted Autumn's permission.

"I don't know what I want," I finally said.

"You should be open to giving and receiving love, son. Autumn would want you to move on and find love again with someone who would make you happy and someone who would make an amazing mother to Marshall."

I mulled over her words for a long moment. She was right in everything she said, but it also felt completely wrong.

"You should see her with Marshall. He adores her as his teacher."

She smiled. "He talks of her often."

"Why do I feel like shit, though?"

She held her hand out, and I placed mine in hers. She squeezed it and smiled. "Because, son, you're human. It's perfectly natural to feel this way."

"She knows about Autumn."

"Good. Does she have a past as well?"

I nodded. "She walked in on her ex cheating on her. She moved across the country to be with him here."

"Ouch," my mom said. "I assume she wasn't ready to jump forward with you either?"

I nodded. "Exactly. We both have our hesitations, but we

also both want this. She's scared to open her heart because of her ex. I'm frightened to give her mine because of Autumn."

"She will always be the love of your life, Noah."

I let another sigh go and pulled my hand from hers. I groaned and pinched the bridge of my nose. "That's just it, Mom."

"What?"

"Autumn was my first love, but Cara..." I lowered my hand and looked into my mother's eyes again. "She's the love of my life. I feel it deep inside me. And right next to it is a black mark from not feeling this way about Autumn."

My mother stood and moved over next to me. She pulled me into her arms and hugged me close. "Oh, son, it's okay. We all fall in and out of love, and when we find our other half, it slams us into a brick wall during the worst part of a hurricane. There's no escaping it or getting around it. If she's the one, you will know it."

I closed my eyes, and a single tear slipped down my cheek. "Thank you, Mom."

"I love you, Noah."

"I love you too." I let her go and swiped at the dampness on my face, then stood. "I'm going to go to bed now."

I finished my tea and rinsed out my cup. Mom took it and placed it in the dishwasher. I left the kitchen and headed toward the room that was mine now if I ever needed it. Marshall was fast asleep in the room that used to be mine growing up.

It still had all my football and baseball trophies, banners, and everything I'd ever earned. Marshall had added his own touch of hanging model planes and a toy fire truck. We had painted the station number on the side with NYFD under it.

I loved my son and would do anything for him, but if

bringing Cara into his life as a stepmother was too much, I would end it. Period. His happiness would come above my own.

I removed my clothes except for my boxers and crawled under the covers. The chill of the fabric was the comfort that always brought me to sleep.

I closed my eyes, and memories of Cara danced across my mind. Dreams would come soon, and I hoped they would be of her, Marshall, and a life we could lead together as a family.

CHAPTER THIRTEEN

CARA

The school season led into the fall season quickly, and it was Halloween week. Halloween was my favorite holiday, with Christmas a close second. I loved everything about it. From dressing up to the trick-or-treaters, it was such a fun day. I should write to whoever comes up with Hallmark holidays and request Halloween be changed from a day to an entire month. I would be recognized with some type of Nobel prize for being a genius.

Why didn't anyone think of this sooner?

I laughed off the foolish dreams and focused on my students. Small hands were cutting out pumpkins, leaves, ghosts, and witches' hats. I had the glue sticks at the ready when a knock at the door caught everyone's attention.

It was volunteer day, so someone's parent was here to help with anything from serving snacks to cutting out pumpkins. I hadn't checked to see who today's volunteer was. Honestly, I'd forgotten to look.

"Keep cutting! We'll be gluing these to our poster boards soon!" I announced and made my way to the door.

Heat rushed my neck and my cheeks when, through the window in my door, I saw the familiar face I looked forward to seeing after hours and on weekends. I twisted the handle and pulled the door open. "Noah," I said in a lower voice and tucked some hair behind my ear. "Is it your week already?"

He nodded. "Good to see you, baby," he whispered.

I bit my lips and smiled. Opening the door wider, I turned to the students and then focused in on Marshall.

"Everyone, please say hello to Marshall's dad, Mr. Hughes!"

Noah stepped past me, and the scent of soot and soap filled my head. It was intoxicating. He wore a lumberjack-style shirt in red and black squares, fitted jeans, and black boots.

"Dad!" Marshall called out.

"Hey, sports fan!" He went to his son and gave him a hug, then messed with his hair. "Where do you need me?" Noah asked me.

Against the wall in the supply closet was what I wanted to say. Instead, I settled on something more teacherly. "Help the students who may be having trouble cutting out the shapes. We'll be gluing everything to poster boards soon."

"You got it. I have mad paper-shape-cutting skills, so you kids watch out!"

A few of the students giggled.

"No you don't," Marshall chimed in. "You can barely cut a straight edge!"

I giggled, then covered my lips with my fingertips.

"Ow, kid. What happened to my wingman? You let me down, man," Noah teased.

"Whatever, Dad. Here, cut out these pumpkins."

I smiled at their interaction. It was cute. When Noah finished the first set of pumpkins, one of the other students handed him white paper and asked for ghosts. He began cutting without drawing anything, and truth be told, they were horrible.

As I made my way around the room, I came up behind Noah while he continued to cut. His blond hair was styled, and his tall, large body was entirely too big for the small chair he sat on. I tried not to giggle when I stepped closer.

"You know," I said as I bent down to Noah, "I've witnessed my five-year-olds cutting better paper dolls from no pattern than the monstrosity you're creating."

"I'll have you know," he started and turned in his too-small-for-him chair and smirked, "I received my masters in cutting out pumpkins from the University of Paper Cutting."

"Daaaad," Marshall said, dragging it out. "No, you didn't. You went to college, then became a firefighter. That's what you said."

"Son, it was a joke. Why are you ruining my style, man?"

I grinned and motioned to Marshall. "I have your back on this one, Marshall. Your father thinks he's so clever. Now, Mr. Hughes, if you will please cut the ghosts like the one Jasmine did here." I picked up the one the student next to Noah cut out as a pattern.

"You can't tell me what to do or how to cut things. I'm my own man," Noah teased.

I laughed. "Well, that's just too bad. This is the only time I can tell everyone what to do and get away with it. My classroom, my rules."

"What does that mean, 'my own man'?" Jasmine asked.

I looked at Noah and raised my brow. "He doesn't like it when I tell him what to do," I answered.

"I don't like it when my mommy tells me what to do," Jasmine offered.

"But do you do it anyway?" Noah asked.

She nodded. "Yes, because if I don't, I'll get into trouble.

She said next time I don't listen, she'll take away one of my dolls."

Noah gasped and covered his mouth with his hands in mock horror. "Say it isn't so!"

It was the most adorable thing I'd witnessed from this man.

Jasmine nodded, and her childlike eyes widened with affirmation. "Yes! I love my dolls, so I listen to my mommy."

"What about you, Marshall? Do you listen to your daddy all the time like you're supposed to?" I asked.

Marshall nodded. "Yep!"

Noah chuckled. "Sure you do, little man."

Marshall side-glanced his dad, then went back to cutting.

I snickered once more and moved toward where the poster board sat. I picked up a few pieces, and when I turned, Noah stood just behind me. His glass-blue eyes bore into my own. I felt the air rush from my lungs in his presence. I wanted to hold him, kiss him, take him into my supply closet again. I wanted to bring him home to meet my family. There was so much I wanted from this man, and he let me in the other night when he discussed Autumn, Marshall's mother.

A part of me wanted to comfort Noah for the loss of his wife. She would always be his first love, where I would be second. And I was perfectly fine with that. In a way, I wish I could have met Autumn, but getting to know Marshall had let me into that part of Noah's world.

The buzzer I set sounded, reminding me that craft time was almost over. The students who were ready to go to recess outside cheered, while others who wanted to continue working on their craft projects groaned. Future artists in the making!

"Okay, students, let's put down our paints, markers,

scissors, and glue. It's recess time. When we return, we can finish up by gluing our cutouts to the poster board. The paint will be dry by then."

Everyone lined up, and Marshall stood at the front as line leader. He motioned the others in their respective places, and when I glanced over to Noah, he beamed with pride. I made my way over to the door when one of my teacher's aides stood at the ready.

Recess was normally my time to catch up on activities while the aides in the classroom managed recess. I could update grades, return emails and calls to parents, and clean up my room. However, today's work would have to wait while Noah Hughes was in my room.

"See you soon, sports fan," Noah called after Marshall.

The students went out, and the door closed behind them. The room fell into silence except for the thumping of my heart in my ears. I stacked papers on desks and closed paint lids. Noah joined me in my efforts, and I casually glanced over to him. He winked as he cleaned up desks. Heat raced up between my legs, and my clit throbbed like a beacon.

I'm here!

Come find me!

I'm yours!

I squeezed my legs together to extinguish the fire Noah didn't realize he'd started by simply winking at me.

"So," he said, "can I ask you a question?" He bent down and quickly jotted something on a piece of paper.

"Sure," I said and tried to look at what he wrote.

He quickly folded it and then handed it over to me.

I took it and held his gaze. "What is this?"

"Read it and find out."

I ripped it open, hoping to read "meet me in the closet." Instead, it had a question and three checkboxes.

Do you like me?
Yes
No
You're hot

I laughed and picked up a pencil from the desk I was near. I scribbled *Meet me in the closet and find out*, then handed it back to him.

He opened it and raised his brows. He met my gaze. "Now?"

"We have twenty minutes."

He chuckled, folded the note, and pushed it into his pocket. "Good, because I only need thirty seconds."

This time I laughed. He was definitely good for more than thirty seconds, and I knew he was trying to be funny, but I couldn't do this during school hours. Hell, I can't believe we did this *after* school hours that day.

The memory erupted a flood in my pussy, and damn it, I needed Noah. Desperately.

"How about after school?" I offered.

"Sounds like a plan," he responded and crossed the room toward me. Noah lifted a hand and ran his fingers across my cheek. "You're absolutely beautiful, Cara. Especially with the swipe of blue across your forehead."

My eyes widened. "What? I smeared paint on myself?" I brought my hands up to see they were clean, and then I frowned. "I hope you're only teasing me right now."

He chuckled with a nod. "Yes, you're clean, baby." He

cupped my cheek and traced his thumb over my skin. Noah began to lean in, and I tilted my head up. Just as he was about to press his lips to mine, movement in the corner of my eye caught my attention.

I turned to look and found Erin watching us through the window of my door. Her arms were crossed over her chest, and she wore a frown of disgust on her face. She moved her head back and forth as if to suggest disappointment.

"Shit," I whispered and moved out of Noah's grasp. I started to walk toward my door, when Erin disappeared down the hall. "Shit!"

"What's the matter?" Noah asked.

"Erin saw us."

"And? Why is that a problem?"

With a sigh, I turned back to him and crossed my arms over my chest. Fear crept into my chest, and anxiety spiked to something I hadn't felt in many years. Last time I felt this way was when I walked in on Jeremy. However, this time, it was Erin who walked in on me.

"I ... You ..." I growled and tried again. "Noah, you need to go. I'll call you later, okay?"

"Umm, sure, all right. Can I wait to tell Marshall bye?"

I shook my head. "It would be best if you leave. I'll call you later."

"Cara," he started and took a few steps toward me.

I held my hands up and shook my head.

"Cara, what happened? Did I do something wrong?"

"We'll talk later, okay? The children will be back soon. Go ahead and leave. Thank you for your time today." I turned away from the love of my life and headed toward the door, then opened it. I glanced down the hallway but didn't find Erin anywhere.

Fuck! Please don't have gone to the principal. Friends wouldn't rat on friends. Even in this type of situation. Right?

"Cara."

Noah stood directly behind me. I felt the heat of his body come off in waves while my entire being grew colder by the second. I closed my eyes and bit back the tears that threatened to expose my feelings.

"Noah, I'll talk to you later. Please just go." I opened the door wider for him and kept my gaze trained on the floor. I knew if I looked up at him, I would lose it and begin to cry.

Noah hesitated for a moment, then did as I requested. He walked past me, and right when he crossed the threshold, I closed the door behind him. Chancing a glance, I looked up and found Noah standing with his back to the door. He had to be confused by the turn of events, but one of the fears I voiced early on was about my job here at my school. It was now possibly in jeopardy, and I had to ensure everything was under control, including my feelings for a man I should not have become involved with.

CHAPTER FOURTEEN

NOAH

Sometimes getting involved with a woman felt like riding a roller coaster. You're up on top of the world, and before you realize it, you're down at the bottom, hoping to build back momentum to reach that peak once more. Once you're there on top again, if you fight hard for it, you can grab hold and not let go.

I had let go once, caused by the downward spiral of losing Autumn. I didn't wish that pain on my worst enemy. I had shoved my life into fighting fires, all things Marshall, and taking care of my mom. It could always be worse, I told myself. But some days, it felt like nothing could get worse.

A few days had passed since I saw Cara in her classroom, when I had volunteered my time. Something had happened that afternoon. She went from warm as sunshine to cold as ice. I knew she had fears, but with me there was nothing to be concerned about. I wanted her in my life as much as she wanted me in hers.

At least that was my hope. Did she want me in her life? She let me in and helped me understand her hesitations, and I let my own walls down. Why change her tune now? What did Erin have to do with me seeing Cara?

With a sigh, I opened my phone when a reminder popped

up. Halloween party tonight down at the station. I sat back in my chair and rubbed my head.

"Shit," I whispered. I had forgotten about the party. It was a costume party along the block of businesses our firehouse was part of. We handed out candy and let the children check out a fire engine. It had always been fun. I knew Marshall would enjoy it.

I wrote a message to Cara.

> *Hey, beautiful. Plans tonight? The station is hosting a costume contest. Businesses on the block are involved. I would love it if you'd come as my date.*

I set my phone down. I closed my eyes, and images of Cara danced across my mind.

The first night together in the cab when she flipped off the driver, I knew I was a goner even then.

The second time at her place, when she wore that sexy number just for me.

The way her eyes widened the first time I walked into her classroom. The fear and the longing all at once.

The evening in her classroom supply closet.

Fuck.

The way she bent over, grabbed her ass, and then spread her cheeks for me. I closed my eyes and rubbed the erection forming underneath my pants. I imagined her here in front of me, on her knees. I unzipped my pants, reached under my boxers for my cock, and gave it a squeeze. It was hard and ready for my woman's mouth. Her lips, slightly full and delicious ... the way she would swallow my head and take my entire length in her mouth.

As I stroked my dick, in my mind it was her mouth sucking me off. I'd fist my hand in her auburn hair and push her harder onto my cock while I fucked her mouth. Holy fuck, it was good. So good.

My balls twitched with the threat of an orgasm, and I wanted her to swallow me. Every fucking bit. And she would. She was my woman, my baby doll, my lady.

"Fuck!" Warmth jetted across my hand and over my pelvis as I squeezed the head of my cock, her lips sucking the last of my come away. I tilted my head back on the chair and groaned out in temporary satisfaction. I wanted more, needed her here with me.

My phone buzzed, and the sound brought me from my erotic daydream. I padded across the floor to my bathroom, washed my hands, and turned on the shower. I went back for my phone and found two messages—one from Cara and another from my mom.

I opened my mom's first. She had come by and picked up Marshall for the day and an overnight stay since my station was having the party tonight.

Do you need me to bring you more candy for the station?

Sure, the more the better. Kids love candy.

I pressed Send and then pulled up Cara's message.

Then it's a date. Is there anything you'd like me to wear?

Well, it appeared what had made her upset enough to rush me from her classroom had since passed. This brought my spirits up. I grinned at the message, then replied.

Lady Godiva?

The bouncing ellipsis moved on the page, and I smirked at the reply she would be drafting.

*That's my costume for later. I have an
idea for what to wear. Will you pick me
up?*

Hot damn. I couldn't wait for tonight. I wanted to see her now.

I'll be by around seven. See you then.

Shower first, then on to Cara's. And I couldn't wait to bring her to the station. Not only as my date but as my girlfriend.

◆ ◆ ◆ ◆

For tonight's costume party at the station, we all wore our uniform pants. I opted for a sleeveless white T-shirt. The overalls to the pants were the added accessory, or so the ladies at the station said.

When I pulled up to Cara's condo, I wasn't sure what to expect. Lady Godiva was a hopeful possibility for later, but what she would wear for the party left me clueless. When the door opened to her building, Cara Murphy stepped out in Mary Janes with over-the-knee white socks trimmed with lace, a Catholic school girl skirt that was seriously short, a white button-down shirt that was unbuttoned to where the shirt tied under her breasts, and a loose tie in the same pattern as the skirt. Her hair was braided in two French braids and tied off with two ribbons. She was so fucking hot. I wanted to stay here and hope she would teach me a lesson in something... anything. I didn't care, so long as she did it with a long ruler.

Spank me, for I've been a bad kid.

I stepped from my SUV and walked around toward the curb as she made her way down the steps.

"Wow..." I felt like the wolf in the cartoons, whose eyes pop out and tongue rolls onto the floor. All I needed now was a loud horn to blow. "You look sexy as hell, Cara."

She pulled out a Blow Pops sucker from her purse, unwrapped it, and popped it into her mouth. Then she slowly pulled it free... her lips sucking around the ball until it made a pop upon exiting. "I have no idea what you're talking about."

"Fuck," I groaned and shook my head. "That's it, we're not going. Upstairs right now."

She laughed and pointed to my car. "Nope. Party first, fucking later."

I wanted to drop to my knees and beg but chuckled instead. "Okay, fine. You win. But damn, baby. Just... damn."

"Oh, this old thing?" She winked and walked to the curb by the passenger side of my ride. "I'm glad you approve."

"The guys are going to have to put me out tonight, because, baby, you're setting me on fire!"

She giggled and climbed into the car. "Good. It's what I was going for."

It felt like the longest drive of my life with my goddess next to me, her tits looking like absolute perfection. We arrived at the station, and I motioned for her to wait.

I made my way around the ride and looked over at the crew. A few gave me raised brows. They knew I had met someone and it was becoming serious. Being the men they were, they could react like I did or keep their comments to themselves. With these assholes, it could go either way. And I loved them all like brothers.

The women in our crew were another story. Jane was married with children, Emily was single and chased women right along with us, and Janel, the eldest, was like our den mother. She took care of us all.

I opened Cara's door, and when she stepped out, she slid into my arms. Her scent of vanilla and cinnamon was like an onslaught of pheromones to my body. My heart skipped a beat, and my dick grew impossibly harder. I wanted to drop to my knees and beg for mercy, then spread her legs and bury my face in her pussy.

Later . . .

She smirked, popped her sucker back into her mouth and, like before, slowly pulled it free. "Don't worry, I'm only practicing for you."

I groaned and rested my forehead against hers. "You're making this very hard for me."

"Mmm, good. I'm glad I make you hard. Now, let's go party." She sidestepped me and waited by the door.

I closed it and turned to take her hand. We made our way to the opened garage and were welcomed with catcalls and whistles.

"They must be whistling for you and your sexy overalls," she whispered.

I chuckled. "Right. Keep telling yourself that."

I introduced her to my crew, and each of them shook her hand except Emily.

"Damn, son," Emily said. "She's too hot for you. I need to take her off your hands for a while."

I laughed and enjoyed the sound of Cara also laughing.

"That's so sweet of you," Cara offered, "but I only spread for my man here."

The men came back with, "Ooohhh!"

I tucked Cara into my side and wrapped an arm around her. "Mine."

Emily chuckled and shrugged. "I eat better."

"Yes, but I have the dick," I answered.

"Trust me when I say mine's bigger." She gave a wink.

Emily was as good at dishing it out as she was at taking it. She enjoyed a good brawl. And she always had our back.

As the party went on, the children of the neighborhood dwindled down to a bare minimum. Marshall and Mom even swung by. Marshall hugged his teacher, but I could see the confusion on his face, wondering why his schoolteacher was at the firehouse. Good thing he hadn't reached puberty, or I would have to face a whole different level of questions come morning.

Mom looked at Cara with curiosity, but I wasn't ready to introduce her. Not just yet.

As we began to close up the garage, I sat down, and Cara came over and took a seat in my lap. She leaned into me and blew gently on my ear.

"I will have no choice but to take you in the engine if you don't stop."

"Oh, don't tease me like that, Mr. Hughes."

My hands gripped against her body in a helpless effort of self-control.

"I've never done it in a fire engine before, Noah."

"Guess what? That makes two of us," I whispered.

I heard the door close to the office. She stood from my lap, and when I took a look around, I found us to be completely alone. I grinned and took the opportunity given to me.

Taking Cara's hand in my own, I led her to the opposite side of the engine from the office. There was a faint light in the garage—just enough to see her in the shadows. I pressed her body to the engine wall and slanted my mouth across hers. I pushed my tongue through her lips, seeking hers. She groaned against my lips and held on to my biceps.

I reached up to the engine door and fumbled with the handle before gripping it and opening it. "Inside, baby. Now."

She grinned and turned to climb inside. Her legs were smooth like silk, and her ass was delicate and begged to be smacked. I slapped her cheek, and she squealed as she climbed in. I followed her inside and closed the door.

The seats were three across with barely enough legroom, but it was just enough for what we needed. I pushed the overall straps from my shoulders and shoved my pants and boxers down to my knees.

She tugged down her lacy undies to her ankles and pulled them off. I maneuvered her over my lap, and she straddled me. I reached between us and lined up the head of my cock to her pussy, and she slid down, hot and wet.

Cara moved her hips in a circular motion, taking me in completely. She was tight and squeezed my cock with each roll of her body. I untied her naughty schoolgirl shirt and moved it apart to expose a perfect white bra. The garment was thin, and her nipples pressed against the barely there material, almost begging to be sucked.

The air in the engine grew warm, and the sounds of our breathing filled the silence. I pushed her mounds together and licked each nipple one at a time. Giving each taut peak attention, I nibbled on them, drawing a gasp from Cara.

She tilted her head back and exposed the length of her neck. I slid my tongue up the sensitive skin of her neck, stopping near her earlobe. I nibbled on it and felt her body shudder. I drew in a sharp breath when her nails dug into my shoulders.

"Damn, baby," I groaned and moved my hands to her ass, cupping her cheeks.

"You feel so good," she whispered. "Never in my life would I think I'd have sex with my hot firefighter in his engine."

"You're riding my engine just fine, baby," I teased.

She laughed a soft giggle and met my gaze. She slowed her movements and never broke eye contact. Our bodies moved as one, giving and taking, pushing and pulling.

I wasn't sure how long I had been blindly moving through my life, but the moment I'd met Cara, it was like I had opened my eyes for the first time. I never wanted to close them again.

"I love you," I whispered.

She smiled and leaned in. Her lips slanted across mine as she kissed me. "I love you too, Noah."

CHAPTER FIFTEEN

CARA

The sun warmed my face and caressed my skin like a soft kiss of radiance. I smiled and stretched in bed, my body waking from a wonderful night of bliss. Last night's Halloween party at the fire station had been fun with the children who came by, including Marshall. It had gotten even better when the party was over. The sex . . . mind-blowing!

As much as I cared about Noah and knew I loved him, loving him came with a lot of responsibility. Noah came with Marshall and the baggage of a deceased wife. Marshall never knew his mother, and I couldn't imagine going through life without knowing mine. It made my heart hurt for both of them.

But was this a responsibility I was ready for? Was this a commitment I was absolutely certain I wanted? It would confuse Marshall to have me as something other than a teacher. And if Noah and I broke up, how would Noah handle that with him?

I hadn't been too keen on becoming a mother. Since the fallout had happened with Jeremy, becoming a mother, a wife—even someone's girlfriend—was far off the menu for me. Until I met Noah. He changed all of that. How? I wasn't certain, but I couldn't imagine living my life without him in it.

But was I ready to be someone's new mom? A stepmom?

With a sigh, I laid my arm over my face and blocked out the sun.

Then the thought of Erin raced across my mind. She saw the vulnerable moment between Noah and me. I considered her a friend, not someone I was just friendly with. I would think she'd come to me first before taking anything up with a higher authority. But had she gone to the principal about my involvement with Noah? I would have to find out sooner rather than later. I wouldn't want to get called out on the grounds of being inappropriate and lose everything I'd worked toward. But would Erin really do that to me?

If you have to wonder about it, she potentially could.

Sometimes I despised my inner voice.

I sighed. I needed to talk to Mom.

She always had the best advice. I could talk to her about anything. When I'd told her I wanted to be a kindergarten teacher, she said it would be perfect for me. And when I'd landed my teaching position at the New Expeditions Elementary School of Science, Art, and Technology in Manhattan, my mother said, "You did good, kid. Never let anyone hold you back. You can be your own worst enemy, but never let anyone force a door closed on you. You push that son of a bitch open and power right through it. You can do anything, be anything."

I missed my mom and hadn't seen her in a while. That needed to change. Thanksgiving break was coming, followed by Christmas.

Would Noah and Marshall go with me? Would they want me to stay here with them?

I groaned and rolled over in bed. Life shouldn't be this complicated.

Make a decision and follow through. Don't worry about what others think.

This was why I did so well being single.

I looked at the clock on my nightstand, and it read nine a.m. I sat up and picked up my cell phone. My mom was central time in Tennessee, whereas I was eastern. I knew Mom was up. I pressed the speed dial for her number and heard it ring.

"Well, hello there, love bug. How's your morning so far?"

My mom was always cheerful. She seldom had a frown. I loved her so much. "Hi, Mom. So far, so good, although it's only been about fifteen minutes."

"You doing okay, honey?"

She always knew when something was up. It wasn't normal for me to call early on a weekend. I held my head in my hand and sighed into the phone. "Where do I start?"

She was silent for a moment, probably hoping I would begin the conversation. I silently prayed she would instead.

"Let's start with his name and where you met."

She knew me so well.

"Well, I can say he's nothing like Jeremy."

"I never liked that asshole, honey. He didn't deserve you, but there was no stopping you from following him to New York City."

I sighed and closed my eyes. She never let me live that down, but it pushed me forward in the direction I needed. I hated that experience with him, but without it, I wouldn't be where I am, and I wouldn't have met Noah.

"Yes, Mom. I know. Thank you for reminding me of that. Again."

I could almost hear her pressing her lips together across the states in a silent mock of "I told you so."

"His name is Noah," I started. "I met him one night while I was out with friends."

"Okay," she added. "Doesn't sound bad so far."

"Right, because I haven't gotten to the juicy good parts yet."

She laughed into the phone. "Then please, by all means, continue."

I told her about meeting him at the bar, then discovering he was the widowed father of one of my students. That we'd kept up our affair, and that I'd fallen in love with him.

"Oh dear," she whispered. "Well, there's just one thing left to do."

"What's that?"

"You need to invite him home for Thanksgiving. I would love to meet the man who has finally tamed my child's heart."

I rolled my eyes. "He's tamed nothing."

"Oh no?" she questioned. "My dear, you've met your match in this man from what I hear in your story. He's a widowed man who's a firefighter, sexy as sin—your words, not mine—and has the biggest heart on his sleeve. He's madly in love with you. Oh, that last part is my words, not yours."

"And he has a son, Mom."

"So what? Is that a deal breaker for you?"

I shook my head. I knew she couldn't see me, but I remained silent for a moment.

"Honey, if you're not one hundred percent certain Noah and his son are for you or you aren't willing to be part of their lives, you need to cut ties now. It's better before it gets too serious."

"Yes, Mom, I know. But that's just it."

"What is that, hon?"

"I absolutely adore his son, Marshall. He's a wonderful kid. When he saw me with his dad at a party Noah had, he didn't really question it. He looked at me, and I could see the confusion, but it was as if he shrugged and thought, *cool*."

"So you can see your life with Noah and his Marshall, then?"

A tear slipped down my cheek, but it wasn't from sadness. It was from joy. "Yes, absolutely. I am in love with him, Mommy." It wasn't often I called her mommy. Only when I felt vulnerable.

"There's my baby girl," my mom said with a larger-than-life smile in her voice. "I need to meet my future son-in-law and future grandchild."

"Mom!" I gasped. "No one said anything about marriage!"

She chuckled, and I could picture her cheeks red with humor. They would always redden when she would joke or tease someone. "Not yet, but I'm positive it's coming. Just be ready, my love. Be ready and open to the idea."

I glanced down at my left hand and tried to imagine a ring on my ring finger. Once upon a time, I wanted this with Jeremy. Then that evil bastard ripped out my heart and beat it with a cleaver.

However, with Noah, my knight who would go to battle for me, his mettle was tested to the brink of devastation, and he came out with his armor tarnished. And it made him the most incredible man in my eyes.

"Cara?" she asked.

"Yes, Mom?"

"Do you love him?"

I smiled and brought my left hand to my heart. "Yes, yes, I do."

"Then you need to figure out what diamond shape you love most, my dear."

I laughed into the phone and swiped at the tears my eyes produced. "How did you know Dad was right for you?"

"I didn't. Not at first. He swore to me that I was born to be his, though. In time, I grew to believe him and knew he was born to be mine."

"Noah was married to Marshall's mother, though. I feel as if I'm playing second fiddle."

"You know, my daughter, we can fall in love many times in our lives. He may have fallen in love with Marshall's mother, but he found you after the ashes fell. Just remember that."

My mother always had the right thing to say regardless of the situation. "Kind of like a phoenix."

"Yes, exactly. And you're just that spark he needed to reignite the flame inside himself. No pun intended because he's a firefighter."

I giggled into the phone. "You should see him in his turnout gear. Man, he's hot!"

She laughed. "Then I look forward to meeting him. Let me know if you're able to come here for Thanksgiving or if it would be easier for me to come out since Noah has Marshall."

I sighed with a smile. "Mom, you're amazing."

"Thank you. And you're just like me, just as amazing. I love you, Cara."

"I love you too, Mommy. I'll let you know about the holidays soon."

"Okay, dear. Bye for now."

"Bye."

We hung up, and I lay back down on my bed. I brought my left hand back up and stared at my ring finger, willing the image of a diamond into my head.

Would Noah ask me to marry him? How would Marshall

react to the news? How would I break it to the principal of the school that I was marrying the father of one of my students?

Well, even though it isn't their business, it could end your fucking career if you come out with this news.

With another long, lung-filled sigh, I turned onto my side, pulled a pillow into my chest, and held it close. It comforted me in the same strange way a child clings to a teddy bear.

My mother's words of advice of long ago rang through my head. "To get anywhere in the world, you need a good purse, great shoes, and at least a hundred dollars in your hand at any given moment."

I didn't think shoes, a purse, and money could get me out of this predicament. But did I even want out? No, not really. I wanted to dive deep and immerse myself in all things Noah. I wanted to be his and him to be mine. I wanted it all, even if it cost me my position at the school.

Noah would be worth it.

CHAPTER SIXTEEN

NOAH

Halloween was behind us, and I must admit it was the best Halloween I'd had in a very long time. My time with Marshall was always amazing, but this time, with Cara, it was completely different. She had a fire about her that could light the darkest of rooms ... just with her smile. She radiated confidence and sensuality. I salivated anytime I thought of her and being inside her. She opened a door to my heart that had been slammed shut after Autumn passed away.

Thanksgiving was on the horizon, and New York City had had its first snowfall. The fires we had been called out to consisted mainly of mismanagement of fireplaces, kids playing with matches and lighters, and the occasional smoker who had fallen asleep with a cigarette in their hand. The latter was more common, but getting called out because children started a fire was something no one ever wanted to attend. It wasn't because of the reckless nature. It was the possibility of finding a child's body in the ashes.

My friends on the police force had told stories of domestic violence calls that resulted in the deaths of the spouse and, more often than not, the children as well. Those are the kind of calls that made your stomach churn, and it took everything humanly possible to not want to strangle, shoot, or just break the neck of the person who would ever do that to a child.

When I saw a child around Marshall's age mixed up in these things, it made me hug Marshall that much tighter at the end of the day. Losing a parent to cancer was one thing. Losing them to violence was something completely different. No child ever deserved that type of treatment.

Padding across the hall at the firehouse, I checked the schedule for Thanksgiving. I typically had Thanksgiving and the day after off by trading working the day after Christmas and New Year's Eve. I was happy to see nothing had changed.

Would Cara be interested in having Thanksgiving with me? Maybe she wanted me to travel with her to Tennessee. I wonder if she had told her mom about Marshall, or even me, for that matter?

It was time to discuss what would happen for the holidays. Being single was easy—come and go as I please, go wherever, do whatever. Now that I was spoken for, it meant inviting Cara, getting her family's approval, my family approving of her ... Sometimes it was all too much. But for Cara? Totally worth it.

I made my way to the locker room. The floor consisted of large checkered tiles of silver and dark gray with a thick red stripe of tiles running down the middle. Three walls were lined with shelves painted red with hangers for turnout gear, space for boots, and an area for our helmets. Above the lockers, a motto was painted for the team across the three walls:

FIREFIGHTERS DEMONSTRATE CONCERN FOR OTHERS, A WILLINGNESS TO HELP THOSE IN NEED ...
THE COURAGE TO PERFORM THE JOB'S DUTIES, TO SERVE UNSELFISHLY WHENEVER CALLED ...
A SPIRIT THAT WAS CALLED UPON WHEN RELIEF WAS NEEDED FAR AWAY FROM THEIR OWN HOME.

I recalled the events that happened during 9/11. I had been sixteen and knew then I wanted to become a firefighter. My mom had called me brave. My dad had suggested I find a different field of work. He didn't want his only son running into burning buildings that could collapse and kill him.

I dug my phone out from my clothes and pulled up Cara's information. I had saved her picture along with her contact information. I loved looking at her image. There were times I felt she could see directly into my soul. I wanted to share the deepest part of myself with her, and in some instances, I had. She knew about Autumn, her dying, and Marshall. Hell, she was Marshall's teacher. She had gotten to know my son in a way no other woman had. She had a huge advantage on that front.

Maybe one day she'd consider him hers as well.

Marriage. Shit, was I ready for that? I loved Cara, I knew that much, but was I ready to give her my name?

With a heavy sigh, I leaned against the wall and continued to stare at her image, when a new message popped up on my phone.

"Speak of the devil." I grinned and opened the unread message from my love.

Hey there, sexy fireman of mine! How's it going today?

I moved my fingers across the screen as I sent a message back.

Not too bad. It's been an easy day so far.
Off in a few hours.

I pressed Send and let my arm go slack. Should I have invited her for Thanksgiving and Christmas? Should I have planned that far ahead and expected her to still be in my life? Shit, we were a couple now. How did I do this without fucking it up?

Hi, my name is Dick. I can't think for myself because I have a Noah. I mean, my name is Noah, and I have a dick.

It used to be so easy for me. Really, it had been. I could stand there and smile, and women swooned and wanted to jump into bed with me. Easy. I might take them home and sleep with them, but I would then forget them the next day. Living was easy until Cara walked into my life. I didn't want to go back to those days. I *wanted* hard. I *needed* difficult. I needed Cara in my life. It felt amazing, and she completed me the moment we first connected.

My phone buzzed, and I brought it up to read her text.

Do you and the kiddo have plans tonight?
If not, I'd love it if you'd come over.

> *No plans, and I can have my mom watch*
> *Marshall. I can be over around nine if*
> *that works.*

The phone showed she was typing a reply, and a second later, it appeared.

Perfect. I'll see you then.

Great.

I paused and stared at my screen, then continued the reply.

*There are a few things I want to talk
about with you. Nothing bad, just a few
things with the holidays coming up.*

*Good to hear. I have a few holiday things
to talk to you about as well. See you then!
Love you.*

Then she sent a selfie of her blowing a kiss.

I chuckled and responded with my own selfie of me with my brows raised, mouth open, and my hand pointing down.

*Send me a blowjob selfie,
and I'll show you my junk.*

I pressed Send and imagined the sound of Cara's laughter. A second later, a picture came through of her holding her hand up and her cheek pushed out by her tongue. The perfect image of a blowjob picture.

I chuckled and pulled my pants out, and as promised, I took a picture of my junk and sent it. I smiled as I waited for her picture back and wasn't disappointed. She pulled the camera back and held it up. The image was of her standing in her bra and panties only, with a pouty look on her face.

*There's only so much I can do without
you. Hurry home, lover.*

Damn it, she was hot. So fucking hot. I wanted to do more than have her suck my dick. I wanted to taste her on my tongue, lick her from clit to ass, then take her from behind. My cock hardened with the anticipation of her being putty in my hands.

> *I'll see you soon. You got me hard.*
> *How do I work now?*

Her response came through a moment later.

> *I would be happy to help relieve some of*
> *that work tension, but you're there and*
> *I'm here. So I'll see you around nine.*
> *Don't be late.*

I groaned and put my phone away before we continued to sext each other. She was amazing—hot, delicious, and mine.

I reached into my pants and readjusted my erection, then thought about baseball, football, soccer, anything to get this hard-on down. Then the alarm bell rang.

Yep, that did it. My erection was completely gone. My teammates came running in, and we all changed into our turnout gear. I grabbed my helmet as we beat feet toward the engine.

"Accident downtown on Essex Street. Pedestrian hit by a cab. The driver is still at the scene. Ambulance and police are en route."

Timing was everything. There were days no calls were received. Those were the best. No accidents, no reports, nothing to worry about. It also meant the days would drag by. We would play chess, perform practice drills, or watch movies.

Then the days that we received back-to-back calls meant we couldn't take a minute to use the bathroom, catch a breath, write up the necessary evil of paperwork. The paperwork could vary between maintenance requests to the station log. A few of the fighters were certified EMTs, including me. If we had to run medical calls, that was a whole new world of paperwork.

We had a rescue ambulance staffed with at least one fire-paramedic and one fire-EMT. We could also run transport as well. Paperwork could take hours. I hoped tonight was not like that. I wanted to get to Cara as quickly as possible.

We ran toward the engine and climbed aboard. I fastened myself in on the seat I'd made love to Cara on. If I were looking for an excuse to regain my lost erection, this would be it.

Please, don't let any of these asshats ask about my night with Cara in the cab. I'll never hear the end of it, and I wouldn't be able to bring her back without someone giving me or even her some shit.

The ride was as quiet as usual, aside from the normal questions.

Who's running medic?

Who's blocking the road?

Who's working with the police and EMTs once they show up?

We all played our own parts, and as a team, we worked well together. The only hiccup that had happened was when one of us fell. Smoke could take a man down faster than fire. Breathing in the smoke could put one under faster than being in a room full of flames.

As we approached the accident, I could see the pedestrian bleeding onto the street. A cab driver stood over him with his hands on his hips. His posture gave off the vibe of the unlucky pedestrian being at fault rather than the driver. Maybe it was. No matter what, you didn't play chicken with cars, especially in Manhattan.

We pulled to a stop, and I climbed out of the cab and made my way over to the victim and checked his pulse. A woman was holding the victim's head.

"I'm Amy and I'm a nurse. I was waiting for the light to turn when this man crossed the street. I don't know if he wasn't paying attention, but the cab driver creamed him."

"Hey, it wasn't my fault!" the driver yelled out.

I looked up at him. "Wait by the car if you would. Police will be here shortly to take your statement."

He nodded and kept by his car.

"Maybe say a prayer that this man lives through the accident?"

"Why? He's costing me money!"

That was all I needed to hear from the asshole who'd hit the man. Regardless who was at fault, this was still a human being.

"Thank you, Amy," I said and checked the man's pulse. It was weak, and more blood was coming from a laceration to his head. "I need bandages!"

Moments later, the ambulance was on scene and took over preparations to get the victim to the hospital. I pulled off the latex gloves, put them into a plastic bag to throw away, and approached the police officer taking statements. It was Officer McNight, someone I had worked with occasionally. Great guy with a fun attitude.

"The driver doesn't appear to have any remorse about hitting the pedestrian," I said. "My two cents, of course, but as he said, it's costing him money to be stuck here and not running his cab."

McNight shook his head. "Well, I can make it really hard on him to make any kind of money today, the rest of this week, or even the next month. We're trying to see if he was at fault or if the pedestrian wasn't paying attention when crossing the street."

"According to the witness"—I pointed to Amy the nurse—"she said the victim began to cross but didn't say it was a walking light."

"Great. Well, that's why we have surveillance videos on the streetlights. Thanks for your time, Hughes."

"You bet. Later." I made my way back toward the engine and grabbed a bottle of water. Our other EMT was working on paperwork, and I reviewed what he wrote up with approval. I checked the time and found it was a quarter to nine.

"Shit," I whispered and reached for my phone. I sent a message to Cara.

> *Hey, beautiful. I'll be late in getting there.*
> *We had an accident to report to. See you*
> *soon. I love you.*

I put my phone back with my other personal items and waited for the accident to wrap up. It looked like the victim was a twenty-nine-year-old male named Timothy Light. No one was sure yet who was at fault. The information would get back to us soon. And if the investigation into the driver turned out to be speeding or running the light, he wouldn't just lose his license. He might serve time.

It was this part of life that I despised and didn't want to let Marshall loose in. At some point, he would grow up and want to go out on his own, and I couldn't protect him forever. But I would for as long as I could.

Same for Cara. As a single woman living in Manhattan, it

was a miracle nothing had happened to her. Arriving on scenes where women had been brutalized always sent a shock to my inner core. I went on autopilot and turned off the emotions. I had to. I had no other choice. Other times, I would return to the station and vomit everything I had eaten that day. It wasn't an easy job, but if I was able to save the life of one person, then it would be worth it.

CHAPTER SEVENTEEN

CARA

I had checked my phone and read that Noah would be late due to a call. No problem. It was to be expected in his line of work. I poured myself a Merlot and took a seat at my dining room table. The placemats were set with dinner that grew cold and candles that were burned almost to the end. I looked like the storybook woman who was on the crest of losing her knight in shining armor. My knight had been kept late was all. Nothing more.

My phone chimed with a new email. I looked down at it and was surprised to see it was from my school's principal. Why would he be contacting me this late on a Sunday night? Then my stomach knotted and dropped to my knees.

The subject was titled *Indefinite Leave*, and the district superintendent was copied.

My eyes blurred with tears, and my heart broke with betrayal.

Erin. It had to be. Who else would do this? But why would Erin go behind my back?

Dear Miss Murphy,

It is with regret we have to inform you that starting Monday, you'll be on leave without pay indefinitely. It has

*been brought to our attention that unprofessional actions
have been taking place in your classroom with a student's
parent. This type of behavior is not accepted in our school,
nor will it be tolerated.*

*You may come to the school when the day ends to pack your
belongings.*

*We regret we have had to come to this decision, and we wish
you nothing but the best in moving forward.*

Sincerely,

Principal Arnold Bishop

I gripped my phone and closed my eyes. A single tear slipped down my cheek.

Three years. Three fucking years, just for it to end this way. No!

I opened my contacts list and pressed Call. The phone rang three times before *she* finally answered.

"Hey, girl. What's up?"

"Erin," I took in a deep breath, then slowly released it.

"Cara? What's going on? You okay?"

I wanted to tear into her, charge her with the guilt of what she had done, but how did I know it was her and not someone else? I bit back my rage and forced myself to calm down. My shoulders and back were still rigid, and my stomach churned as if someone had poured acid into it.

"I just received an email from Principal Bishop." I hated doing this, but I needed to know if it was her or someone else. "Care to tell me what's going on? Because after this email, I'm honestly confused."

There was an uncomfortable silence on the phone for what felt like an eternity, when in reality it was maybe thirty seconds.

Erin sighed into the phone. "It's not like you left me a choice, Cara. You were basically opening your legs for Noah Hughes on your desk in front of the kids!"

I gasped. It *was* her, someone I trusted. I sagged in my chair, and the tears shot past the gates of "oh hell no, she doesn't deserve your tears" barrier. "How could you?"

"Put yourself in my position, Cara. How would you feel if you saw me with someone in my classroom, all but fucking?"

"Number one, that never happened in front of the kids and you know it! Number two, what I do with Noah Hughes is none of your fucking business. But now that you've taken it upon yourself to make it your business, I hope you're happy."

"Jesus, Cara, don't hate me. It's business, not personal."

I laughed, but there was no humor to it. "Wow, Erin. Just wow. You know, I don't hate you. I'm just disappointed you turned into everything you said you'd never be."

"That's not fair," she retorted.

"Isn't it, though? The worst thing about betrayal is knowing that it was done by someone you trusted the most."

"Whatever, Cara. I'm done here."

Before she could hang up, I yelled, "No, you don't get to hang up on me. Let me tell you what's going to happen. You lied. You flat out lied, and you know it. You have no idea what I have with Noah or if we have anything at all. I'll give you one chance to make it right with the principal and superintendent. If you don't, you'll be hearing from my lawyer. Slanderous accusations follow people around."

"Oh yeah? You wouldn't sue me."

"Wouldn't I, though?" I had never used my family's money as a bargaining chip or held it over anyone's head, but I wasn't above doing that now. "Make the call, or you'll see me in court."

"Go ahead and threaten me all you want, Cara. It doesn't matter. What's done is done."

Before I opted to hang up on her, I pulled one more string. It had been a sore subject with Erin when we had first discussed it, and we never spoke of it.

The tenure in our positions put one of us into a leadership role for the school. This role meant decision making, and this would eventually lead to the role of principal, maybe even superintendent. Erin salivated at the opportunity to run things, but it had been my name the principal had always called on.

"If you wanted the leadership role this desperately, I would have dropped out of the running and given it to you. If this is what this is about—"

"It's not about that, but thanks for thinking so wholeheartedly of me. Nevertheless, it's mine now anyway."

"Well, fuck you and your sour life. I hope karma fucks you in the ass." I hung up and chucked my phone across the room. It bounced off the wall and spun on the floor. After I threw it, I cringed that I might have broken it. When it simply continued to rotate in circles on the floor, I sighed and rested my forehead on my arms on the table.

How did I get here? Why did this happen? Why Erin? Did she want my job that desperately? Had she wanted me out of the way and felt I was that much competition? Did a part of Erin possibly want Noah for herself?

Noah. Hell. I can't do this tonight.

With tears now flowing in a steady stream from my eyes,

I stood and crossed the room to where my phone sat on the floor. I picked it up and growled at the crack that had formed across the screen.

I pulled up my messages to reply to Noah's.

> *Noah, not tonight. Something's come up.*
> *I'm going to be out of pocket for a while.*
> *Please, don't call me or come over. I'm*
> *sorry. It sucks, but I need space right now.*

I stared at my phone until the letters began to morph into different figures through my tears. I pressed Send, set the phone down, and then leaned over the table and blew out the candles. I pressed my palms into the wood of the table and hung my head low. My shoulders shook as I sobbed.

I'd lost my job, everything I'd worked toward, and lost who I'd thought was one of my best friends. If hell was being betrayed by someone you trusted, then this was my own personal inferno.

Luci purred and rubbed his body against my ankles. A growl roared from my lungs and turned into a scream. Luci, my poor cat, ran from the room. I'd make it up to him later, but right now, I needed to get control of myself before I ruined more than my career.

The silence of my home was filled with my sobs until my phone rang. I didn't want to talk to anyone, but if it was my mom, I was willing to make an exception. I looked at the caller ID and cried even more when it was Noah's name. He must have read my text and now wanted to talk.

But I couldn't.

I wouldn't.

I didn't want to go through another heartache. It was better this way. I was better off alone than to share my life with someone who would ultimately break my heart. Erin had. Why wouldn't Noah?

I let his call go to voicemail, and then he called again.

And again.

And again.

At some point, my voicemail would be filled. Would he continue to call or just stop? Would he give up on us? On me?

Why not? Everyone else had.

"Fuck this," I mumbled and left the table with my phone sitting on it. As I turned the corner, it rang again—no doubt Noah calling—but I didn't want to talk to him. Not now. He would convince me to let him come over. I'd worked hard on building my protective fortress, and in no time, Noah had managed to knock it down. Well, damn it, consider it refortified with new cement. No one would ever get through it again.

I was done letting people in. I was done trusting.

I was just done.

I walked into my bedroom, and Luci sat on my bed and lifted his head. He meowed at me as if asking, *What the fuck is your problem?*

I climbed across my bed and lay next to my cat. Luci had been through a lot with me. He had been there during my breakup and recovery from Jeremy, and here he was again, my confidant through Erin and Noah.

Although Noah did nothing, in time, I'm positive he would have. Why wouldn't he? Everyone shit on me.

Don't have such a pity fucking party. Noah has given no indication he would do this to you. He opened his heart to you. Why would he do that and then turn around and smash yours?

I wanted to yell at my inner voice to shut up, but the point was made. He gave his heart, and it was me who smashed it. I was a despicable human being.

A new onslaught of tears started, and I pulled Luci into an embrace. He resisted but eventually realized he wouldn't win and gave up. He lay there with me while I sobbed, and after a long moment, he began to purr.

I pulled my legs up and curled around my cat while my heart broke into a million pieces. I needed a do-over button. I needed a door to escape. I needed someone to hug me.

I needed Noah.

CHAPTER EIGHTEEN

NOAH

I had learned years ago through a nasty breakup—before I met Autumn—that rejection didn't mean you weren't good enough for the other person. It meant the other person didn't notice who you were and what you could offer in the relationship. I didn't want to admit that Cara couldn't see the potential between us, but I knew something had happened. But what?

I thought back to the day when I volunteered at the school. She rushed me from her classroom after Erin had seen us. Afterward, we continued on as if nothing had happened, and I had accepted that instead of asking questions about what might happen.

I looked at the calls I'd made to her. If I were being honest with myself, I was becoming a borderline stalker. Who called someone this much?

A man in love with a woman rejecting him, that's who.

I wrapped up the night and decided to drive to my mom's. She had Marshall. Since my evening events had changed, thanks to Cara, why not just call it a night?

I stepped out of my car, and the wind chill reminded me winter was nearly upon us. I was still dirty from the night and needed a shower. My plan was to clean up at Cara's and have her in there with me. Now I'd go it alone.

Reaching the front door, I unlocked it and let myself in. My mom was in the living room with a lamp on, reading. I shut the door behind me and took a few steps in.

She looked up and did a double take. She put down her book and frowned. "Noah, what happened?"

"What makes you think something is wrong?" I closed the distance to where she sat and stood over her. "Everything is peachy."

She lifted her brow, then reached her hand up for mine. I took it and lowered to my knees. My heart was breaking, and I had no idea why Cara had a sudden change in hers.

"What happened?" she asked. "Talk to me, son. I can see it written all over you."

I sighed, and my body sagged. I sat on my heels and shrugged. "Everything happened, Mom. Everything."

"Was it a rescue mission tonight gone wrong?"

I shook my head. "No, not this time. It's ... it's Cara."

A moment of silence passed between us when my mom touched my chin and lifted my face up. "Tell me what happened. How can I help?"

"You can't," I whispered. I told her about Cara's text and my calling her a number of times. "I don't know what else to do."

"Have you thought about going over there? Bringing some food with you?"

"No, she doesn't want to see me."

"That's her head. Her heart will be different. Trust me on this. Go pick up her favorite food and drive over there. Knock on her door until she answers. She'll let you in. Talk it through. Whatever happened doesn't sound like it had anything to do with you. Something drastic may have happened that shook her soul. It's up to you to find out why and be there for her. Don't worry about holidays, family time, all that crap. Go to her and just be."

"Just be . . . what?"

"Whatever she needs you to be. Be vulnerable, just like her. I can almost guarantee the two of you will be just fine. She just needs to take a breath."

"How can you be so sure?"

"Well, son, last time I checked, I'm a woman. I know how we think. We think with our hearts. You men think with your dicks."

"Oh hell, Mom, I don't need that right now."

She laughed, and it brought a smile to my lips. She always knew how to get me to laugh, even in the hardest of situations. I loved her so much for that.

She scooted forward and pulled me to her. I wrapped my arms around the first woman I'd ever loved, my mother. I couldn't imagine this life without her, and she was right. I needed to go to Cara.

"Thank you," I whispered.

"You're welcome, son. Now"—she pulled away and fanned in front of her face—"I love you more than life itself, but son, you reek. Go shower before you go sweep your lady off her feet."

I chuckled and nodded. "Yes, ma'am."

♦ ♦ ♦ ♦

It was almost midnight. Chinese food in one hand, my heart in the other, I approached Cara's condo building. The downstairs door was locked unless you had a key for entrance to the building. This could be a potential problem.

Did I ring the bell in hopes she'd let me up?

Stand like John Cusack and blast "In Your Eyes" with hopes no one called the police? Man, I could just picture the ration of shit I'd get down at the station.

Or I'd get lucky and be standing here when one of her neighbors left. I grinned and grabbed the door as a blond woman stepped out. She looked me over with a smile and paused as if to ask a question—one I answered before she began her first word.

"My girlfriend lives here."

"Oh right, I think I've seen you around here. Too bad. If you weren't spoken for—"

"Thank you, I'm flattered." I rushed through the door as it closed behind me and headed up the all-too-familiar staircase to her door. Just behind it was the woman of my dreams, my son's teacher—the lady who'd stolen my heart.

I swallowed the heavy lump in my throat and took a chance. I knocked three times on her door. Looking to the ground by the doorframe, I saw a shadow move across the entrance. I smiled. She was home.

"What are you doing here?" Cara asked through the door.

"Please, open the door?"

"You didn't answer my question."

"You didn't give me much of a choice in what to do about us, Cara. Please, open so we can talk. Look"—I held up the bag—"I brought your favorite. Szechuan chicken."

"That's not my favorite."

I lowered the bag and looked at the peephole in the door. "Please, baby, open the door."

The peephole grew bright again, and then the locks

clicked. She opened it just enough to where I could see her.

She wore old, ratty, flannel pajamas, her hair was in a messy bun, and her cheeks were splotched from crying.

And she was absolutely beautiful.

I smiled and leaned against the doorjamb. "Hi."

She lowered her gaze and whispered, "Hey."

"Can I please come in?"

She nodded and opened the door wider, then stepped back toward her couch. She sat down and tucked her legs under her body. I closed the door, flipped the locks, and removed my jacket, then padded over to the couch. I placed the food down and sat next to her. I reached for the tissues on the table and handed them to her.

Cara began to cry again. I reached around her shoulders and pulled her toward me. She didn't fight it. Instead, she leaned into my chest, and I held on to her as she shook. I felt my T-shirt dampen from her tears.

"Start at the beginning. What happened?"

Cara sat up and wiped at her eyes, and then, grabbing a tissue, she blew her nose. "I'm . . . I'm sorry, Noah."

"Don't do that. I'm fine. Just tell me what happened." I brushed some loose strands of hair behind her ear and waited for her to start talking. I would wait all night if that's what it would require. I didn't care. I loved her.

"The day I rushed you from my classroom?"

I nodded for her to continue.

"My so-called best friend, Erin, told the principal you and I were fucking in my classroom."

I raised my brows. Well, we had fucked in her classroom, but never anything out in the open or in front of the children. Not even hand holding.

"The principal took it up with the superintendent. I'm on indefinite leave without pay."

"Oh shit," I whispered.

She nodded. "I want to talk to my principal about it and make my case that they don't have grounds to fire me without proof."

"I agree."

She looked up to me, and her bottom lip trembled. "The fact that one teacher informed the district that another was putting her students in danger was enough for indefinite leave."

"How was our seeing each other putting any of the students in jeopardy?"

"It was about Marshall," she told me through a hiccup.

"My son? What does Marshall have to do with us?"

"That's just it," she started and wiped at her eyes. "According to district rules and regulations, my relationship with you would jeopardize him. I broke the rules getting involved with you."

I let a long sigh go and recalled the first time she had told me we needed to do the right thing and not see each other again. But I was a greedy bastard and had wanted more of Cara.

"I'll not apologize for chasing you, Cara. You're a wonderful woman, and I love you. I don't regret that at all, but I do feel guilty about the fact you've lost your job because of us."

"We agreed we'd keep this light. We agreed to that, Noah." She stood from the couch and began to pace. "We weren't going to let things like feelings get in the way, yet here we are. And now . . . now I've lost everything I've worked for. All because of a good piece of ass."

That hit like an arrow to the chest, and Cara held the bow.

It hurt like hell. "You don't mean that."

She met my gaze, and I could see the hurt in her eyes—the torment, the deception of her friend. "I called the principal and asked to be reassigned instead of being placed on leave. He said he'd ask to meet with the school board on my behalf, but he doesn't have his hopes up. Even if successful, I'd be starting over. Everything I had is now gone thanks to this shit between us."

"Stop." I stood and took a few strides around her living room. "Just stop before you say something you'll regret."

She shook her head, and a new rush of tears streamed down her cheeks. "I need you to leave, please. Just go, Noah. Get out. Just leave, please."

"Cara." I tried to reach for her. When she didn't move, I took a step closer and took her hand. "Please, don't," I whispered. I held her close, cupped her face, and wiped her tears with my thumbs. "Please." I lowered my forehead to rest against hers.

She sniffed and gripped my wrists. We were both falling, and we grasped each other for strength. I needed her as much as she needed me, and I was determined to prove this to her, even if it took the rest of my life.

"Noah," she whispered through a sob. "Please."

"Yes, baby?" I looked into her eyes. I wanted to kiss her, hold her, make love to her, just to prove I was here and on her side.

"Leave."

"Baby, please, don't—"

"Leave. Don't make this harder than it already is. Just go." She pulled my arms from around her, made her way over to the front door, and opened it.

"Cara, don't do this."

"Noah, please just go!"

I closed my eyes and fought the pain of the tears that surfaced. Against my better judgment, I nodded, then walked past her. Just as I crossed the threshold, Cara closed and locked her door. I leaned against it and felt the pressure of the door move, probably from her leaning against it from the other side.

As I slid down to the floor, I imagined she did it with me and we managed to stay connected. The wood between us was only two to three inches thick, but we were miles apart in this moment.

I rested my arms on my knees and let my head hang low. Where did I go from here? Calls, food, and showing up on Cara's doorstep did nothing to help regain her favor. She was hurting, and she'd need time to heal, but she needed me as well. It was just a matter of time before she saw that.

I only hoped when that time came, it wasn't too late.

CHAPTER NINETEEN

CARA

When I'd met with the principal this afternoon, I wasn't sure what to expect. He requested for me to remain in the teachers' lounge until the school day ended. Thankfully, that was only about an hour. I thought of how everything had come to a head with Erin, Noah, my career as a teacher ending… It wasn't supposed to end this way. I was a fighter and always had been, but I also knew when to accept defeat. When your boss tells you that you're out, there's not much negotiating around that.

The bell rang for the final call. End of day had arrived. There were the sounds of students bustling in the hallway, lockers opening and closing, gossip being passed from one student to the next over who was wearing what, and who was picked for teams. When the door to the lounge opened, I didn't expect *her* to walk in.

"Oh, I didn't realize you would be here," Erin said, then turned up her nose to run the water at the sink.

Snake. That's exactly what she was. She wanted my job, wanted the involvement with the school, and eventually wanted the recommendation to be superintendent. None of it was guaranteed unless you proved yourself. Even then, it was a crapshoot.

I stood, crossed the floor to the counter, and folded my

arms over my chest. "Why'd you do it?"

She flinched, not realizing either that I would dare ask her or stand so close—probably both. Erin shrugged. "All's fair in love and war, Cara."

"Who's at war here? I was never out for you."

She turned off the water and yanked a paper towel from the dispenser, then turned to face me. "Let me see if I can put this into terms you can understand."

The words offended me, but instead of retaliating, I listened, my hands in fists.

"You are rich. Like, filthy rich. You've never had to want or need for anything. You get the men—all the men!—all the time. You never have to work for it. They just drop to their knees and become dumb to whatever goddess pheromone you wear. Same for this job. I don't know who you fucked to get it, but it ends now."

I slapped her. It happened before I realized what I had done, but the shock on her face made me proud I did it. My palm stung, and it was glorious.

"First of all, I've worked for everything I have ever received. My family's money had nothing to do with my career as a teacher. Secondly, I don't get all the men. How they fall to their dumb knees over my, as you say, 'goddess pheromones' isn't something I do or don't do. I'm real and don't play games. Try it sometime. The slap was for the job. I never fucked or sucked anyone to get to where I was. I did that all on my own. You'll do good to remember that next time you go accusing somebody."

She rubbed her cheek, and if stares could kill, I'd be dead. "Whatever. I won this time. So go pack your shit and get out of my school." She turned on her heel and left the lounge. I silently hoped others would see her red cheek and wonder who she'd pissed off to get it.

I leaned against the counter and took one last look around. It would be the last time I saw this place. In a few minutes, the principal would be here to walk me to my old classroom. I only hoped the students knew I loved them and that my leaving had nothing to do with them.

Moments later, the door opened and Principal Bishop poked his head in. "Let's go."

Together, we walked the halls one final time toward my old classroom. The last time we'd walked this path, it was my first day. I glanced over to him, then back to the floor.

"Normally, I wouldn't ask someone who was on indefinite leave to wait in the teacher's lounge, but something told me I didn't have to worry about you."

I thought of the slap I'd given Erin. "No, sir, nothing to worry about."

"Look," he started and turned toward me. "I'm sorry things ended this way, but we have rules for a reason. Dating a student's parent is not acceptable behavior for our teachers. Nor is having relations in your classroom."

I thought about his last sentence for a moment. "Who, may I ask, informed you I was having relations in my classroom?"

He wouldn't look at me, so I pressed on.

"Was it Erin? She came out and told me it was her who ratted me out. So if it was her, I'd like to know."

"You know I cannot confirm nor deny that accusation."

I sighed with a nod. "As I suspected. Perhaps you should further investigate matters before shooting first and asking questions later."

"Pardon me?"

"Listen," I turned to face him this time. "You came to me with this information and never gave me a chance to defend myself. You fired me before hearing my side of the story. It's not fair."

"And it's an employment-at-will state. An employer may terminate an employment relationship at any time for any reason."

I nodded. "Yes, and unless a law or agreement provides otherwise."

"What are you getting at, Miss Murphy?"

"I'm saying, you should have investigated the source further. Did you bother to check any video camera feed from the halls for proof of these so-called relations? Just don't be surprised by what she may try." Thankfully we didn't have cameras in the classrooms yet, but I imagined that would be changing soon.

He frowned and remained quiet for a moment. "What do you think she'd try?"

I shrugged. "I don't know. It's an employment-at-will state. I'm not willing to share that information now that I'm no longer your employee."

"That's not very nice, Miss Murphy."

"Neither is accusing me of violating the rules without proof." I turned toward my old classroom and felt sadness creep over me. "Will there be anything else, sir?"

Principal Bishop sighed behind me, and then he muttered, "No."

I looked around the room, and my eyes burned from the threat of tears. I loved my students and loved teaching. I sure as hell didn't do it for the money. I loved their little minds and how they absorbed everything they were taught. They were our future, and my goal was to help broaden their horizon as much as I could, while I could.

I made my way to the desk, pulled the chair out, and sat down. I glanced around the classroom and could almost hear the voices of the students talking, laughing, and reading stories—even Marshall, with Noah across the room cutting out pumpkins and ghosts.

Noah. Great, adding him to my torment was not needed in this moment. I opened my top drawer and removed my personal items so I could place them in the box conveniently left for me. I opened my file drawers and saw the old copy of *Wuthering Heights* I took with me to every classroom. I smiled and picked it up.

Randomly, I flipped through the pages and landed on a passage.

"I have not broken your heart—you have broken it; and in breaking it, you have broken mine."

With a sigh, I closed the book and let the tears flow free. I had been a right foul shit to Noah last night.

At least I didn't walk in on him fucking someone else. If I had, would it have been easier to break things off with him? Yeah, it would have, because Noah didn't do anything to deserve this. I loved him but let him go. What the hell was wrong with me?

After I packed up my belongings, I looked over my classroom once more.

"Miss Murphy?" Principal Bishop called.

I wiped my tears away and, with a sigh, stood from my old desk. "I'm fine," I mumbled and walked past him into the hall.

As soon as I walked out the doors for the final time, the sobbing started once more. Right now, I felt utterly and completely alone.

CHAPTER TWENTY

NOAH

When you wanted something, you fought for it, tooth and nail, blood, sweat, and tears. You fought for it until it became yours. If it wasn't meant to be, you let it go. But you had to know, once and for all, if it was worth fighting for.

If the woman wasn't the one, I wouldn't fight for her. But Cara? She was the one. I knew she was, and she knew I was her equal as well. She might not want to admit that, but she knew, and I would do everything I could to get her to declare it as the truth.

I got into my SUV and held on to the steering wheel. I was on autopilot. I drove without thinking or feeling. Her place was my destination, but I was at a loss about how I planned to prove to her we belonged together. I loved Cara, and I didn't want to live this life without her, but if she insisted it was indeed over, I'd have no choice but to accept defeat.

But failure was not part of my vocabulary.

I turned down her street and, with a sigh, parked. I gripped the steering wheel and willed myself to exit my SUV and go to the woman I loved. My heart raced, and my ears thumped with each beat. I began to perspire. I should feel a chill, but instead, on this cold fall day, I was completely numb.

I turned off the ignition and felt my stomach lurch.

Fuck.

I wasn't good at this. Being part of a couple wasn't something I'd wanted after Autumn, but for Cara, I was willing to put forth the effort. She would need to meet me halfway. I opened the car door, and a brisk breeze blew around me. I welcomed the chill, for I needed it with the heat my body was producing from the nerves plaguing my mind. I looked up at her window. Was she looking down at the street? Would she see me? Should I go for holding up the radio while it blared "In Your Eyes"?

Just go to her, you idiot.

Taking the steps up to her building, I stared at the call pad. Her name was the third one, listed simply as Murphy. I reached for it and gently touched it with my finger but didn't press it. Not yet.

Was she home?

Would she see me?

What if she sent me away?

What if you just man up and press the fucking button?

As much as I hated my inner voice at times, it never steered me wrong. I pressed her call button, and it buzzed. I waited what felt like an eternity.

"Yes?"

I exhaled the breath I'd been holding when I heard her voice. I pressed the button once more to talk. "Hey, Cara. It's Noah." I let the button go and waited.

It felt as if the world turned toward me and watched, waiting to see what happened. Would she open the door, or would she tell me to leave?

The door buzzed. I quickly grabbed the handle and felt my mouth pull into a smile. This was at least the first step. The door closed behind me, and it was then that I finally really felt the chill of the weather. My body shook, and I moved my hands up and down my arms to produce heat.

I took the steps two at a time and climbed to her floor. Her door was slightly opened. I began the walk to her condo when Cara popped out.

She wore the same flannel pajamas as the other night, but this time, her cheeks weren't flushed, and her eyes weren't red. Her hair was pulled to a side braid. And she looked perfect. My perfect woman.

I stopped when our gazes met. She hypnotized me in the best way. I couldn't move or even blink, for fear if I did, she would disappear.

Cara raised her brows. "What are you doing?"

"I—" I wasn't sure what to say, so instead I willed my feet to move. Thankfully they did. I made it to her door. "Hi."

She opened her door fully and clasped her hands in front of her body. "Hello." Cara lowered her gaze to the floor, then leaned against the doorjamb.

"I've missed you," I said.

She lifted her eyes and met mine. "You have?"

I took a step closer. "Of course I have. I love you."

She sighed and lowered her gaze once more, then motioned with her arm for me to enter her apartment.

I stepped past her and waited for her to close the door. She flipped the locks and hesitated by the door. I wanted to go to her, turn her to face me, but I held my position. When she did turn around, I wanted more than anything to press her body to the wall and make love to her, but wants needed to wait. Right now it was about needs.

I needed Cara in my life.

I needed her to believe that.

I needed her to listen.

She motioned to the couch in her living room. I took a seat, and she sat on the opposite side, putting both space and silence between us, and it was as thick as pie. I needed a knife to cut through it to get to her—to my love.

I flinched when her cat, Luci, jumped up on my lap. He meowed and looked up at me.

"Well, Luci likes no one but me. He never comes out for anyone, so this is a first."

"Can I pet you?" I asked Luci, half expecting the cat to answer. Instead, when I raised my hand to offer it to him, he sniffed it, then rubbed his face against my fingers. "I take that as a yes." I petted his head, then scratched behind his ears. Luci then lay down in my lap and purred.

I raised my brows and looked at Cara.

"He definitely likes you. He won't even come out for my mom."

"Wow," I whispered and continued to scratch behind his ears. I took this as a sign to continue with Cara. "So, listen, there are some things I need to get off my chest."

"Same here. Can I go first?"

I nodded, adjusted myself on the couch to face her, and helped Luci get into a comfortable position.

"I'm so sorry for how I treated you. You've been so wonderful to me, and you didn't deserve that. I hope you can forgive me?"

I smiled. "Of course. There's nothing to forgive."

Cara smiled at my words. "Oh, I'm not done," she continued. "As you know, I lost my job."

Guilt punched me in the gut once more. "I'm so sorry."

"Thank you. I told you before that someone told the principal we were involved and accused me of putting Marshall in a bad situation."

I felt my cheeks heat with anger. Mess with me, I might be able to let it slide. Mess with my son? All bets were off. "We both know that's not the case. We also didn't exactly come out to anyone, so how did they find out?"

"It doesn't matter. They found out."

I sat back for a moment and thought about her words. She was terminated because she dated one of her students' parents. There was only one person I was aware of who knew we were involved, if at all. It was the teacher-friend Cara had mentioned she was with the night we met.

Cara warned me this could potentially be an issue, but we decided we knew best. Maybe that hadn't been such a great idea. I didn't regret any of this, but I hoped Cara wouldn't hold resentment against me for the turn of events. I'd pursued her. I'd wanted this. I didn't force her hand, but I might as well have. I wanted to feel guilty, but anger made a fiercer presence.

I frowned and wondered if I mentioned Erin, the teacher she had worked with, if it would upset her. Would she deny the accusation? "Was it your friend Erin?"

She lowered her gaze and didn't confirm or deny my question.

I knew it. "Why?" I asked. "What did she have to gain to throw you under the bus like that?"

"It doesn't matter," she offered.

"Yes, it does matter. She had to have a reason."

Cara sighed and pinched the bridge of her nose. "Yes, it was Erin. She's been gunning for my job, and I didn't realize it until I was terminated. I was going to be offered the job of running our department, and eventually I was going to make a play for superintendent. To do that, you need credentials from the school—credentials I was on the verge of gaining. Apparently she wanted the same, so she decided the best way to get it was to go after me. No matter the cost."

"So, she thought shitting on your friendship would get her these credentials and this opportunity?"

Cara nodded.

"Well, that's a shitty way of going about it."

"Yep. I warned the principal about his actions as well. That putting me on leave because of Erin's accusations will come with repercussions."

My brows rose. "What kind of repercussions?"

"Just that if Erin went after me for my job, what's to stop her from going after someone else's? Like his. I also think it would be a good idea to write a letter to the principal, making it clear that in no way is Erin allowed anywhere near your son, for any reason."

She was right. I nodded. "I'll definitely do that." I paused and considered my next words. "Well, I came over today to beg for you to come back. And I'm not above getting on my knees and pleading with you."

Cara fidgeted with her fingers, and then a smile tugged the corners of her mouth. "I would love to see you do that." She raised her gaze and met mine.

It was good to see her lighten up. She needed a laugh, which I hoped I could give her. She needed someone to lean on. I longed to be her person. "Which part? Beg or get on my knees?"

"Both, please?"

I smirked and picked up Luci. "Sorry, kiddo. Your mama

needs me to plead for my life."

Luci meowed at me, then jetted away as soon as I placed him on the couch. I stood and took a few steps closer to Cara, then got down on my knees. I took her right hand into both of mine, then brought it to my lips.

"Please, baby girl, please forgive me and my foolish ways." I closed my eyes and brought our hands to my heart. "Please, I beg you with all things on this green earth, to take me back. Please"—I did my best impression of a minister cleansing demons from a person's body on television—"let our love be enough to cut through the curtains of this universe and allow me to hold you in my arms once more." I held our hands up to my forehead. "Please, woman, I'm begging you here, please! I love you, Cara Murphy."

I brought our hands back to my heart, and I took a chance to look up into her eyes . . . and found her in tears. I frowned and moved to the couch next to her. This wasn't the result I was hoping for. "What the hell did I say? I'm sorry, baby. I didn't mean to make you cry."

She shook her head and took her hand back from me. She wiped her eyes and hiccupped. "You're apologizing for something you didn't even do. You're begging me to come back, when I left and pushed you away. It should be me begging for you to take me back."

I reached for her and cupped the side of her face, then swiped at her tears with my thumbs. "You know, I'm not above begging and a blow job."

She stopped crying and looked at me with a confused expression. It took only a moment before her frown shifted into a grin, and Cara then began to giggle. "How do you do that?"

"Do what, baby?"

"Take a serious conversation and make it a joke?"

"Oh, this isn't a joke, baby. I want you back, and if I'm not mistaken, you want me as well. All I'm saying is I'm down for a blow job."

She rolled her eyes and laughed, then sniffed. "I love you too." She climbed over me and straddled my lap. She pushed her fingers through my hair and tugged my head back. Cara then slanted her lips across mine and kissed me.

I cupped her ass and squeezed her closer to me. Our tongues tangled in a dance of seduction. Her lips were soft, and she tasted of cinnamon.

She let a soft groan escape, then mumbled, "I missed you so much. I'm so sorry."

"I'm here now," I told her. "And I'm never going anywhere again."

"Good, because I don't want you to go anywhere without me."

I stood, Cara's body in my arms, and carried her toward her bedroom. I laid her back against her bed. Her legs remained tight around my waist, and I pressed my erection against her body, the friction drawing a moan from her.

I didn't want to stop kissing her, but fuck, we needed to remove our clothes. I reached up and grabbed my T-shirt, yanked it over my head, and tossed it.

Cara pushed against my chest, and I stood over her. She sat up and unbuttoned her flannel top. Her breasts were bare underneath, and I couldn't wait to taste her mounds once more. She lifted herself up and removed her bottoms, then lay naked for me on her bed.

I grinned and placed my hand over my mouth. I shook my

head and closed my eyes.

"What's the matter?" she asked.

I opened my eyes and moved my hand. "I'm just grateful that all of this is mine."

She smirked. "Then come and take it."

Quickly I removed my shoes, socks, and pants, then my boxers. I returned to Cara and pushed her back against the mattress again. She moved her legs up around my waist and lifted her head up to kiss me.

"Don't you dare hold back," she whispered. "I need you inside me, right now, Noah Hughes."

A groan escaped me, and I reached between us to line up my cock to her pussy and pushed. I filled her instantly, and she arched her back. Fuck, she felt amazing around my dick. Her walls squeezed my manhood as I pulled out and thrust back in.

She grabbed hold of my shoulders, and her nails dug into my skin. The sensation of her holding on hurt and burned in the best way possible. If she were marking her territory or staking a claim over me, I welcomed it.

"I love you," I grunted as my body moved in rhythm with hers. I slipped my fingers around her throat. She met my gaze, and her lips parted with a gasp.

"I love you," she whispered between thrusts.

I squeezed slightly on her throat, and she moaned louder, her pussy tightening around my cock. "You like that?"

"Yes," she groaned. "Yes, harder, baby. Harder. Make me yours."

I didn't hesitate. I pulled back and slammed back deep inside her. Cara's back arched, and she gasped hard against the slight strangle I had on her.

"Pull my hair," she requested.

I let go of her throat and pressed my hand to the bed. I fisted my other hand in her hair and yanked it to the side.

She gasped, and her pussy tightened around my dick. I tugged her hair again, this time harder. Cara screamed out, and I moved my body faster, my cock pushing deeper inside her.

"You. Are. Mine," I grunted with each thrust in her ear, then nibbled on her earlobe.

"Yes!" she yelled out. "Yes!"

My balls tightened, and the familiar warning I was about to come surfaced. "Baby," I whispered, "hold on . . . hold on. Don't shatter for me yet."

"I'm trying," she cried out. "Oh shit, Noah. I need to, please."

"Fuck," I growled. "Come for me, baby, come with me. Now."

Cara's body went rigid, and I thrust once more as warm liquid spilled from me inside her. "Holy hell." My breath came out in pants. I felt a warm rush come from her, soaking my pelvis and balls.

Cara panted, beads of sweat on her face, as her chest rose and fell. She held on to me, and her legs began to turn soft and limp. "May I ask something?"

"Anything." I looked into her eyes and slipped my lips across hers. In this moment, I knew she could see directly into my soul.

"Can we fight more often?"

I chuckled and pushed my dick inside her once more. "Anything you want, baby."

"I only want you, Noah. I want my life with you and Marshall. I need you both. I love you so much."

I teased my nose across hers, then kissed her once more. "I love you too. And we're yours, baby. I'm yours."

EPILOGUE

CARA

A year had passed since I'd met Noah, and it had been a roller coaster of a ride. I had continued teaching and considered furthering my studies into special education. I picked up a few books from the local library and read articles on how teachers have accommodated to curriculums, autism, and nonverbal students.

Noah and Marshall moved in with me in my condo. He had put the place he had with Autumn up for sale. Per Noah's request: "It didn't feel right moving you in when we could start something new." I agreed with him, but I also wouldn't have minded living there. I think if Autumn and I had met under different circumstances, we would have become friends.

I had seen a few pictures of her, including those of their wedding day. Marshall had her eyes. I could see a part of her in him every time we spoke.

As for Marshall, he enjoyed having me around and called me "his dad's girlfriend." And I was just fine with that.

Today, I'd gotten a call from Principal Bishop. He'd requested my attendance back at New Expeditions School. I wore a red-colored dress with a white overcoat. Christmas was coming soon, and I felt like Mrs. Claus. I had the best man in the world and was gaining a new son. My life felt complete.

I made my way into Mr. Bishop's office and noticed he was not at his desk. Instead, I went over to his assistant, Mrs. Beverly Scott.

"Hi there," I said, and Beverly looked up.

She smiled and stood from her seat. "Well, look who the cat dragged in! Cara Murphy, it is *great* to see you!"

"Well, it's great being seen. How've you been?"

"Oh, I'm good." She motioned to a chair for me to sit in. "I know you're here to see Principal Bishop, but woman, I need to prepare you for what you're in for." She lowered her voice. "You remember Erin Malone?"

I lifted a brow. "Yes."

She smiled and pressed her fingertips together. "Miss Malone has had a misunderstanding of how things work around here."

"Oh? What does it have to do with me?"

Beverly leaned in. "Let's just say that she has been removed from the grounds and will never teach again."

What the hell did she do? I tilted my head, confused. "Can I ask what happened?"

"Since the investigation is now over, yes. I can tell you she tried to blackmail Principal Bishop into giving her what she didn't deserve. When a position to run the kindergarten program up through third-grade classes became available, she was quite upset that she was not selected. So she decided she would come in here and offer a sexual trade in exchange for the position."

My eyes widened. "No, she didn't!"

"She most certainly did. She had it in her head that you apparently did this. When Bishop marched her out of his office, he told her that her belongings would be packed for her and to never return."

"Oh my," I whispered and sat back in my chair. "Then why am I here?"

"I'll be happy to explain that."

I turned around in my chair to find Principal Bishop behind me.

I stood and turned to face him. "Hi. Thank you for calling me."

"Thank you for giving me a chance to speak with you directly. Now, if you wouldn't mind?" He motioned toward his office.

I looked over to Beverly and mouthed *thank you*. She returned it with a nod and a wink.

Principal Bishop and I went into his office, and he pulled a chair out for me at his conference room table. He took a seat and crossed one leg over the other.

"I'm a man of integrity and can admit when I've been wrong."

I sat forward in my seat. "Okay? Well, what can I do for you?"

"It's more like what I can do for you."

I was curious about what he wanted to offer.

"Since I overheard your conversation with Beverly, you're aware of the situation."

I nodded. "It's too bad how it all came about."

"Truly," he said and folded his hands in his lap. "I'm prepared to offer you your job back, full tenure, and the promotion to run the kindergarten through third-grade classes here at New Expeditions. You'll take on the art division and receive a generous bump in pay, full benefits, and a bonus for coming back."

I widened my eyes, completely caught off guard. "I

appreciate the offer, and trust me, I want to say yes, but you and I both know I broke the rules when dating Marshall's father, Noah."

He nodded. "I'm very well aware of that. But that school year is now behind us."

"So, have the rules changed?"

"Kind of. If a teacher is found to have been dating a student's parent, we've made a rule change to move that student to a new classroom."

"That's all?"

He nodded. "That's all."

I smiled. This was what I wanted—tenure, to run the department, and in time, make a run for superintendent. It was all on a plate just waiting for me to say yes.

But this involved more than just me.

"Would you mind giving me one minute, please? I need to make a quick call before I give you my decision."

"Of course. Take all the time you need."

I nodded, pulled out my phone, and called Noah. I stood and left Mr. Bishop's office while the phone rang.

"Hey, baby," Noah answered.

"Hey, yourself. So I'm here at New Expeditions." I told Noah everything I was being offered. "What do you think?"

The line was silent for a moment. "Well, this is your decision, baby, not mine."

"I'm aware of that, but this affects you as well."

"I think you should go for it."

"I'm glad you said that. Thank you. See you later tonight."

"You got it. Love you."

"Love you, too." I hung up the phone and returned to Mr. Bishop's office.

"Well? What's the verdict?" he asked.

"I'll accept on one condition."

"Okay?"

"If there are any allegations, they'll be investigated before any decisions are made."

"Agreed," he said. "Anything else?"

"Yes. I need you to be aware that Noah, Marshall, and I are now living together."

He nodded and offered a letter packet. "Thanks for letting me know. Inside is everything we talked about, as well as an offer letter. I'm happy to have you back at New Expeditions, Miss Murphy."

I was happy to be back too. I wouldn't trade this life, this misadventure with my firefighter, for anything in the world.

NOAH

Everything had fallen into place. Cara got her job back with the school and received full tenure. Marshall and I moved in with her, and he got a new room out of it. He loved the space and living in a condo.

He also seemed to enjoy having Cara around as a motherly figure. And her cat took to Marshall like a new best friend. Marshall asked why a boy cat would be named Luci. I loved his innocence and hoped he held on to it for many more years to come.

Tonight would be a game changer. It wasn't Christmas, but it might as well have been. Tonight I planned to propose to Cara.

I had talked to Marshall about it just after we moved in.

"How would you feel if Cara would become your stepmother?" I had asked.

"I like her, Dad. I'm not sure I'm ready to call her Mom, though."

I'd smiled. "You don't have to until you're ready. She'll never ask you to do it, either, unless you want to."

He'd nodded. "Then I'm good with it. I love our new place, and you smile more with her."

It had warmed my heart, and I knew Cara and I were doing a good thing.

The evening had approached quickly, and now dinner was finished. We all sat at the dining room table. I looked over to Marshall and winked. He winked back and took his dish to the sink, then took off for his bedroom, Luci right behind him, chasing his heels.

"What was that about?" Cara asked.

"No idea what you mean." As soon as Marshall was out of sight, I reached for Cara's hand. I brought it to my lips and kissed the top of it. "We've been through a lot, baby."

She smiled. "Yeah, we have."

"I'm not good with speeches, but I am with begging." She giggled, and I stood from my chair. "Cara Murphy." I bent down to one knee and tugged a ring box from my pants pocket. "Will you do me the honor of becoming my wife?"

Her eyes widened, and when she didn't say anything, I continued.

"Please, baby?"

She blinked, then fell into my arms and screamed out, "Yes!"

I chuckled and hugged her to me. I never wanted to let go. "I hope the ring meets your approval. My wingman helped me pick it out."

She pulled back to look at what was in the box. It was a teardrop-shaped yellow diamond surrounded by rubies set in a platinum setting. A tear slipped down her cheek, and I smiled when she held her hand out.

I slipped the ring onto her finger, and she hiccupped.

"Thank you. I love it."

"I was hoping you would. These are the colors of fire, because baby, you set me alive when we met, and I haven't been the same since. I want you to be mine officially. I love you."

"I love you too."

Marshall peeked back into the room. "Can I come back now?"

Cara laughed, motioned him over to the two of us, and embraced him in her arms. "I love you too, kiddo. Thank you for helping your daddy pick out such a beautiful ring."

"You're welcome, Miss Mur— Wait, do I still call you Miss Murphy?"

"You can call me Cara, or, when you're ready, Mom."

He smiled and rested his head on her chest. My heart swelled with love, and if I wasn't careful, it might burst into flames. Good thing I was a firefighter.

MORE MISADVENTURES

Callan Walsh kicks ass. In fact, he's famous for it. As one of the brightest up-and-coming stars on the MMA scene, he's an absolute beast in the cage...and out. Everything he's trained for has brought him to this moment. Going toe-to-toe with reigning champ Xavier Gray will make or break his career. Nothing can distract him from his lifelong goal. Nothing. Until he meets...his opponent's little sister.

Josie Gray is hell on wheels, gorgeous AF, and has a mouth that doesn't stop. The reluctant reality-television star is every man's dream, but she's about to become Callan's nightmare. Tired of being in her brother's fight-club entourage, Josie desperately desires her own life out of the limelight. Her loyalty to family keeps her tangled in faux fame, but what she feels for Callan is the realest thing she's ever known.

Sparks fly when Callan comes to Josie's rescue, leading to an all-consuming fire after a single night together. Forever is right at their fingertips, if only everything—and everyone—wasn't working to keep them apart. Will Callan and Josie fight through family ties to come out on top? Or are they both caged into lives they never wanted?

VISIT MISADVENTURES.COM FOR MORE INFORMATION!

MORE MISADVENTURES

**VISIT MISADVENTURES.COM
FOR MORE INFORMATION!**

ACKNOWLEDGMENTS

Heather Ray and Martha Frantz — You were with me every step of the way. I owe you so much. Thank you.

To the team at Waterhouse Press — Thank you for making this process seamless. You've been incredible!

To Victoria Blue — Thank you for all of your advice, letting me pick your brain, and just being one of the most amazing people I know.

And finally, to my husband, John — You've been so supportive. You've been my rock. Thank you. I love you.

ABOUT JULIE MORGAN

USA Today and award-winning bestselling author Julie Morgan holds a degree in computer science and loves science fiction shows and movies. Encouraged by her family, she began writing. Originally from Texas, Julie now resides in Central Florida with her husband and daughter, where she is an advocate for children with special needs. She can be found playing games with her daughter when she isn't lost in another world.

Visit her at JulieMorganBooks.com